About the Author

Born in London, Michael is a businessman and financial adviser. Married, he lives together with his wife in the lovely Berkshire countryside where he likes to write. When not either working or writing Mike as his wife calls him is usually found helping out with her horse business.

To my wife Lindsay for her encouragement and also to of her mother Eileen without whom this may never have been published.

Michael Middleton

SHORT STORY COLLECTION

AUSTIN MACAULEY
PUBLISHERS LTD.

A CIP catalogue record for this title is available from the British Library.

ISBN 9781787101340 (Paperback)
ISBN 9781787101357 (E-Book)
www.austinmacauley.com

First Published (2017)
Austin Macauley Publishers Ltd.
25 Canada Square
Canary Wharf
London
E14 5LQ

Acknowledgments

My colleagues at work for reading my various drafts and putting up with the distractions.

The team at Austin Macauley for having the courage to support me.

Direct Action

It wasn't remotely clear whether the farmer was going to shoot me with the shotgun or not. What was clear is it was pointing directly at my midriff and whilst I knew little about guns I knew enough to realise if he decided to shoot me I was in a world of trouble, or another world altogether.

I was assuming the man was a farmer, he looked like a farmer. Well, he looked like he worked on the land, his face weathered by exposure to the sun and the elements and his frame sinewy with no excess weight, his hands appeared worn and hard, much like his expression. My assumption was also based on the fact I had just stumbled out of a barn and even I was sharp enough to realise it must have been his barn I wound up in last night.

When I found the barn sometime in the night I got in to escape the rain; I was soaked, tired, dirty and not the least sober. Fortunately for me breaking in was not necessary, a side door was wide open, if it hadn't been I would never have got in at all. I had no recollection how I came to be floundering across a muddy field. It was a mystery; after all I had been on a tarmac covered lane for seemingly ages after leaving the pub. But then my brain was destroyed by beer and a heap of other booze that I cannot name. As usual with these things it had seemed a good idea at the time, but right now it was starting to look like the worst idea ever.

Amongst many things to escape my attention in the dark was the proximity of the barn to the farmhouse, barely 20 yards. Quite what alerted my presence to the farmer I have no idea, but when I stepped out into bright sunlight he was standing right where he was now with his 12 gauge, at least that's what I guessed it was, pointing directly at me.

So far he was a man of few words and courtesy of my messed head I was struggling to come up with anything to say. Though it was safe to assume a cosy chat was not high on the list of probabilities for the next few minutes.

Eventually he broke the silence, if not eloquent at least his question was both easy to comprehend and direct.

"Who the fuck are you?" he said.

My mouth was already dry from last night and the limited moisture I might have been able to muster a few minutes earlier had dried right up thanks to having a gun pointed at me. Not something I was used to, so I just made an incomprehensible grunt. The farmer's vocabulary clearly extended further than his first question, but not by much.

"What the fuck are you doing here?" he asked, my capacity to reply being as useful as earlier I simply shrugged.

"Are you taking the piss?" he continued. "You do know I am holding a loaded gun don't you?"

Now he was beginning to demonstrate he had a wider grasp of the English language. "So try answering me, what are you doing here?"

He could also speak without expletives so maybe I had not stumbled into a gangster farmer, maybe just one who was frightened to see the mess I was walk out of his barn first thing in the morning. I was not quite as tall as a rugby lock forward, more like a flanker, but I am not small. My nose looked like it had connected with something hard, which it had, before immediately spreading itself across most of my face and if the mud did not obscure it I had an ugly scar that ran down from my left eye across the cheekbone.

The scar however was a neat straight line created by a surgeon who had removed a rapidly growing cyst that might have been threatening my vision. It certainly made me look fairly ugly, not that I was remotely pretty before the surgeon got to work; the scar made me look like the bad guy from a 1950s Pinewood film. I was told it would begin to lose its bright red appearance in time.

"I' m sorry," I began, both words coming as a croak, "I was just taking shelter from the rain." Perhaps it was the pathetic sound of my voice or maybe he realised I meant him no harm as his shoulders visibly relaxed and the gun lowered a little. I'm sure if it went off now my legs would be in a mess, probably worse than my face but I could live with being ugly and mobile; I had no wish to be an ugly cripple so I raised my hands part in some form of pointless self-defence and half like I had seen in countless old westerns over the years.

"I was lost and pretty drunk," I said, before adding, "completely rat arsed actually."

"Where'd you come from?" he asked.

"Dunno, left a pub in a village and stumbled out on to a road, turned into a lane and then somehow ended up in a field. When I saw this barn I thought I had found the Ritz compared to a night under a hedge."

He lowered the gun further, thankfully it was now pointing at the ground. His hard eyes never left my face though, his expression never changing.

"You want a drink?" he asked. My reply was simply a nod. The good news was he clearly figured the threat level was gone as he hefted the gun and broke it open before popping it on his shoulder and turning around to walk away. "This way," he added, half turning his head back towards me.

I followed him the short distance across the track that was actually the drive up to the front of the farm. The barn entrance I had stepped out of faced north west, the late summer sun was beginning to gain height away to my right in the east, the front of the farm house facing directly towards it. The house and what was supposed to be a front garden but looked more like an overgrown meadow was bounded by a wall that had seen better days. The front of the house looked like it had not been tended by anything other than weather in fifty years, much like the farmer.

We went to the rear of the property, a rickety gate giving way to a small rear garden where at least the patch of grass had been cut. The doorway he led me through went first into a dilapidated lean to come porch from which could be found the kitchen. There was a traditional range to the right and the walls were lined with cupboards but it was hard to imagine they contained anything as the work tops were covered in boxes of breakfast cereal, biscuits, tins and packaged sliced bread. The sink was full of dirty dishes.

In the middle of the room was a table that could easily sit eight people and he invited me to sit before opening the cupboard immediately above the electric kettle. This disproved my theory that all the crockery was in the sink as I could see a couple of chipped mugs and a few plates. He took one mug out and rinsed one from the sink before making tea. He didn't ask me what I wanted but I was in no place to complain.

To my surprise he made the tea in a pot rather than straight into the mugs. He put the mugs, tea pot, some milk and a sugar bowl on the table before turning and hesitating briefly. He pulled open a drawer before quickly shutting it and delving into the sink. Clearly all the cutlery was in the sink. He rinsed the recovered spoons before putting them on the table. He sat down opposite me.

"I'm Charles Ashton, though most people call me Charlie," he said. "What do I call you?"

"Adam, Adam Pierce."

"Well Adam Pierce, I've never shot anyone before but you got close to being the first," Charlie Ashton said. "Thought you might be one of those Carter people always round here thieving and hassling us." He poured us both tea as he spoke. In contrast to his earlier aggressive tone his voice was softer, the West Country accent more in evidence.

"No sir, not me," I said, "and thank you for not shooting me by the way, and for the tea." A smile of relief crossed my face.

He grinned back before continuing as though we had known each other for years. I suspect he spoke to everyone that way, either that or he had no one to speak to. "Those people are a wretched nuisance, first they bought an old farm property up the road with only a small amount of land then started buying land all round us. They want some of mine out the back here," he said, pointing over his shoulder with a thumb.

"They have a small parcel of land behind it and I think they want to build on there." As he spoke his expression became saddened. "Soon after they moved this way, I found out they are developers, they have done similar things all over the south west."

"Why not sell?"

He looked at me as if I Was an idiot. "What? Sell? My grandfather started this farm, even if I wanted to I couldn't sell it."

Whilst I had only come from the barn to his kitchen I got the sense that he was alone. Telling his age was difficult but either he had no children to leave the farm to or they had made themselves scarce. Either way it was hard to see much of a succession plan in place.

"Who follows you then?" I enquired.

The sadness returned to his face, his eyes suddenly becoming a little moist. He drew in a deep breath before continuing.

"I have two children," he said, "my daughter is married but sadly very ill, her husband is her carer." He paused briefly, "And my son has gone, he used to work here with me, but we fought once too often and he just left."

Not being a therapist I had no idea what to say so said nothing.

"I think he'll come back, but I don't know for sure."

We sat in an uneasy silence for a few minutes, before he stood to pick up the tea pot.

"More tea? What about something to eat?"

On the last point I thought he'd never ask, rude of me to presume I guess but I was starving and hadn't eaten since lunchtime the day before.

"Yes please," I said, at which he began sorting and washing out bowls from the sink, which he placed on the table before putting boxes of cereal on the table. Followed by bread, jam and butter. Nothing looked that clean, but I didn't care.

We ate in silence before he stood to make a fresh pot of tea. Once seated again he resumed his questions.

"So which pub were you in Adam and how come you were so drunk?"

I wanted to say don't ask but given I was drinking his tea and eating his cornflakes I guessed some sort of response was called for even though it was going to sound pathetic and in no small amount embarrassing.

"I think the pub was called the Rose and Crown, no idea where it is or quite how I found it, it wasn't the first I had been in."

In fact I think it was the third, but I'd lost count. So I told him about my day, it had started out fairly bad and

17

gone further downhill rapidly. The cause was a girl. Not being the world's best looking guy and never being great with women I had been flattered when I met a girl at work. I was or rather I used to work at a caravan and camping site in Devon. It was the second summer I had spent there, the money wasn't great but the cost of living was pretty much zero and there was nowhere to go and nothing to spend money on unless you wanted to visit Devon's tourist attractions. I had never got to know any of the guests before Janine; she was single and uncomfortable being the sole single girl among her group of friends down for a week's holiday from Bristol. Her attention flattered me; I went out a couple of times with the gang then she and I on their last night went out alone. The evening was great, she was both interesting and interested, not something I had experienced before. I tried to drag the evening out but eventually we had to go back to the site. I walked her back to the site and even managed a good night kiss. Naively not realising it was also meant to be good bye from her stand point.

The following day after a night spent thinking about Janine and not sleeping I decided I would go and ask to see her again. I was shocked to discover they had packed and left before I started work at 7 am.

I would happily accept the observation that I was not the most intelligent person on the planet, but even by my standards the next thing I did was dumb. Plain stupid really. I walked back to my simple digs, packed my rucksack with the few things I owned and walked out. Before I travelled to Bristol I went to the office and checked the register, made a note of Janine's address and set off in pursuit. As I said, stupid.

Finding her was not at all difficult, she lived in a ground floor flat, one of two converted from a Victorian terrace in the Staple Hill area of Bristol. As I had to catch two buses and a train to get to Bristol by the time I walked up the hill toward her place she would have been home a good two hours. My arrival was not the only surprise she got, I was the second, the first it turned out was her boyfriend, who had been at home to wait for her. The same boyfriend who had walked out two weeks earlier meaning she was alone on the camping trip. To say she was not pleased to see me was a major understatement. Her boyfriend wasn't too happy either but he took one look at me and decided he would let her negotiate. I was two sizes bigger than him, plus the nose and scar made me look like someone to be feared, which was sometimes very handy, if not entirely accurate.

I sighed as I said to Charles, "So hopefully you can see why I ended up on a bit of a bender."

"What now?" he asked.

"To be honest I don't know, I have nowhere to go, no job, or at least I assume I won't be welcome back at the site and I haven't enough money to travel back there to find out."

"I could do with some help here if you don't mind a bit of manual labour?"

"Generally no problems there, but I might have a bit more strength tomorrow," I said with a faint laugh. It wasn't difficult for him to tell the state I was in. Something about his question and the tone relaxed me a bit and I drank the tea readily. Fortunately he noticed me empty the contents of the mug and he refilled it from the pot. It might not have been the best tea in the world but to me right then it was the best drink there had ever been.

"I don't know anything about farms and animals," I said, "I might not be much use to you really."

"You'll be a big help, believe me for my age I am pretty strong but moving some of the equipment round here and handling bales of straw and things soon wears me out."

I thought for a moment, truth be told thinking wasn't my strong suit when trying to combat the mother and father of all hangovers, but even in my state I recognised a good offer when I heard one. So I accepted on the spot.

The next two days were spend spent learning all manner of things, from the simple shifting bales of straw by hand to driving an old Ford tractor. Charlie showed me how to clean the cattle pens after fixing the slurry cleaner to the front of the tractor and swapping that round for the front loader with front forks on it to lift the round bales of straw and heavier bales of silage.

Milking time was my first ever contact with any animal other than a family pet and I was both amazed by the cows marching into to the milking parlour without fuss or prompting and terrified by their presence at the same time. They were truly remarkable creatures. In sharp contrast to everything else the milking machines were spotlessly clean and state of the art. Charlie showed me how to fit the automatic teats and how to avoid a kick which cattle were apparently prone to dispense from time to time.

I threw myself into my new surroundings and barely noticed the scruffy bedroom and the state of the bathroom as I collapsed each night with exhaustion. Charlie was not a gourmet cook but he could manage a half decent stew which was a significant improvement on my staple of beans on toast. We ventured to the local supermarket to stock up on the standard items in his cupboard and on one occasion we stopped at the local pub for both a beer and a plate of fish and chips. That I was welcomed back into the Rose and Crown I took as evidence that my behaviour on my previous visit was not as awful as I had feared.

For the next two weeks life went along and was as enjoyable a period as I could recall. I even became moderately competent with the tractor and other machinery on the farm.

Life had settled into an enjoyable pattern of work and despite myself and early misgivings I was thoroughly enjoying not just the work but Charlie's company. My only reservation was the knowledge this could not last forever in fact I was increasingly wondering what I was going to do next.

The last two years whilst working on the caravan site I had largely saved my earnings and together with the odd labouring job had used the money to live through the winter. Now that I had thrown that away I was unclear how I was going to manage through the next winter. One thing I knew for certain was that I was unlikely to be able to stay here throughout that time. It wasn't something that Charlie and I had discussed but it was beginning to feel to me like the elephant in the room. I was just not sure how, when, or where to raise the matter.

Given what had happened in the last month I probably should have worked out that something would hit the fan sooner or later. Ever since the first morning Charlie had only mentioned the Carter's once, it was almost as though they no longer existed. Whatever threat he thought they posed had somehow been mythical and I for one assumed his reaction to finding me that day was just the over sensitive behaviour of a lonely old man who's imagination had begun to get the better of him. In my experience it can happen when the only person you have to speak to is yourself.

I could not have been more wrong.

My first experience of the Carter's was to some degree innocent enough. Charlie wanted to move his small herd of steers from one field to another where the grass was lusher; pasture rotation as Charlie informed me. He had the cattle purely for fattening and then they went off to market he told me, something he had started to do after a disastrous bout of foot and mouth disease some years earlier which had badly impacted his diary herd, a herd he was not keen to expand. Being that he was alone I could see the sense in that, the twice daily milking was surprisingly hard work for me let alone a man I figured to be twice my age.

We had to move the steers down two small lanes, the first was fairly straightforward as not only was the lane narrow but there was high hedging to both sides preventing any risk that the young bulls would seek to go their own way. Getting them to the field gate however was less straightforward. Charlie had me use the quad bike to ride cowboy fashion behind the herd, moving from side to side driving the cattle towards the gate, to make life easier we had moved the electric fencing that he had been using to move the cattle from one side of the field to the other making sure of the most efficient use of the land, not a blade of grass wasted. We used the fencing to create a funnel and a small stockade close to the gate. Once they were in we would close the rear by moving the fence in behind them.

I was bizarrely terrified although I had largely mastered riding the quad, I had never tried to herd cattle. Once we got going though I found it far easier than I had feared and began to feel like a character in a John Wayne western. Charlie did warn me that the steers could be a lot less predictable than their older female companions heading for the parlour. On that point he was spot on as given even the merest opportunity one young steer would make a break for it. Lose him and half the herd would bolt in whatever direction they felt like. I had wondered why Charlie had moved the steers up the field away from the gate rather than start them at the top and move the sections down each day, that was until he pointed out that he had to get them in here on his own so at one time or another it was always likely the whole field would have to be covered, either coming in or out. So with my help it made life easier. I had no idea how he had proposed to move them if he had been alone. I left the question unasked.

After 10 minutes of chasing backwards and forwards , I was actually grinning like an idiot, I had not had so much fun in years.

As we got them closer to the narrow end of the funnel Charlie lifted one end of the fence out from the ground. Each post had a spike on the bottom and a small piece of steel set at right angles to the upright to use to press the spike into the ground with a foot. Waving me to the far side of the funnel Charlie moved with a speed that shocked me, not quite Olympic sprinter but remarkably quick for an elderly man. Before any of the cattle could even think to look behind for an escape route he was standing next to me on the quad with the herd now contained in the temporary stockade.

With cheeky grin Charlie said, "Now for the difficult bit."

"How's that?" I asked.

"Well for a start you need to leave the bike here as the next bit can only be done on foot. I will walk in the front and you follow behind, I don't want you spooking them with the bike 'cos if this lot starts running they won't stop, they'll just run over me like a rugby maul and I will be at the bottom. Ok?"

Now he had me worried, if I screwed up he gets trampled and badly hurt, or worse. Responsibility and I had never been close bed fellows, not killing someone was about as much as I could possibly comprehend. Charlie went on."Don't look so worried. Just walk gently behind them use your voice the way you have been doing with the cows and if needed give them a tap with this," he said handing me a four foot length of stick, "just try not to panic them"

With that he walked round the outside of the stockade, pushed the gate into the lane open which in turn created a neat barrier so at least they could not turn left. Then he opened the electric fencing and called out to his cattle. I have no clue what he said, it was some sort of high pitched yell, that sounded to me like, "Ay ay." With that he turned his back to the herd and walked off down the lane, without any help from me the steers followed, at first some started to trot but as they ran into the hedge on the other side of the lane they slowed to a more modest pace and like a file of school children and followed Charlie up the lane.

"You're like the bloody pied piper," I called out to him, given his lack of response I assumed he couldn't hear me as my cheeky insights rarely passed without a rebuttal. Charlie might be a simple man, but in his case simple did not mean dim. In fact his mind was razor sharp and sometimes so was his tongue.

We negotiated the first lane with ease. As we turned to the right things began to get more interesting. First, Charlie had to continue to lead but also ensure that the herd turned right up the second lane and not left as though heading back to the farm. Since he had not shared with me how he proposed to achieve this as we drew closer to the turn I began to worry as I had visions of having to get past part of the herd as it galloped away in the wrong direction.

As we got closer to the turn Charlie slowed his pace. He moved to the left hand side of the lane and just ahead of the turn dipped into the hedging. He came back out grasping a handle with two parallel lengths of wire attached to it before bolting across the lane. On the other side he anchored the handle onto something I could not see and was back at the front of the herd before I had walked another five yards. This guy was incredible I thought. But on reflection I guess he had been doing this for an awful long time so he was bound to know just what to do and when. To me it looked pure genius.

Unfortunately, as we moved into the next lane we lost the hedge to the left. Our only defence was a narrow ditch, narrow enough that the cattle could hop over with no real effort. I wasn't sure what would happen if they tried to jump and ended up in the ditch as it was a good six feet deep in some places. The only saving grace was the water in the bottom looked very shallow.

Charlie had already instructed me to stand on the rear left flank of the steers and not to risk panicking them at all. If they were to get over the ditch the square open field at the other side was about 60 acres, or to the likes of me around a quarter of a mile in each direction. A bloody big space to lose 50 steers in to use Charlie's words. To make matters worse the crop in the field was not Charlie's so wrecking it was to be avoided.

Despite my fears we navigated the lane without a hitch until the last twenty yards. Charlie's yell of anguish was easy to hear. The cattle stopped dead in their tracks as did I. Although I could see Charlie I could not see what had caused him to call out. Clearly it was not life threatening as in the next instant the air turned blue with a curse laden invective from Charlie. I wasn't at all sure what to do. After a few moments he appeared to calm down a little although his vocabulary remained that of the army barracks.

"The fuckers," he said, "the absolute fucking wankers."

This time he actually scared me a little so my response to him probably sounded slightly frail. "What is it?" I asked.

"Those bastard Carter's have blocked the bloody gate," he called back.

"Can you shift it?"

"Not easily and not without risking this lot running off," he replied. "We've got more chance if you can get this crap out of the way," he said point to his left, "and I manage the cattle. Can you get to the front?"

Not without getting in the ditch or the field opposite I thought. "Sure," I said.

"Best be quick in case the cattle get ideas about pissing off back up the lane," he said.

I leapt over ditch and scrambled to the front as rapidly as I could. Then I saw the problem. Stacked neatly on the field side of the gate was the biggest pile of empty wooden pallets I had seen anywhere other than a transport yard. There were three neat piles butted up against each other completely blocking the gate. I couldn't count precisely how many in each stack but they each stood at about six feet, smaller than me but a good enough obstacle for the herd.

To get in the field I had to climb on the gate then onto the pallets and drop to the other side. Fortunately the pallets were not heavy and with plenty of space to re stack them I was able to get the whole lot away from the gate in a little over five minutes. I was sweating heavily by the time I was finished. I pushed the gate open into the lane and could not see Charlie anywhere. Luckily I could see lots of cattle. Then I heard a sharp shout to my right and looked to see Charlie bring two potential runaways back to the herd. I had no idea how he had stopped the rest following. Given that Charlie was not out of breath I guessed they had not got far in any case. I had to close the gate again to let the three of them back past and give a couple of the steers a hefty slap to make room for the two returning runaways. As soon as they were passed I re-opened the gate, looking across the lane I saw Charlie scrambling along the bank to the back of the herd.

Another ten minutes passed before we had them all secure in their new field and Charlie had to sit at the gate for a few minutes. He was out of breath now. I wasn't sure if it was exertion or stress or a bit of both.

Looking up at me Charlie said, "Now you can see what I'm up against."

I said nothing in reply but merely nodded and thought to myself if he had been here alone he would have been in a lot of trouble.

We gathered ourselves and made sure the cattle were secure in the field and walked back to collect the Quad bike. Charlie told me to leave the electric fence for now so we rode the bike back to the farm with Charlie taking the risk of riding as pillion passenger. He looked very tired and suddenly quite old, the issue with the pallets had clearly upset him more than I realised.

I made a pot of tea in the kitchen and Charlie just sat down and watched in silence. For a man used to doing absolutely everything his acceptance of me using his kitchen was in sharp contrast to his normal behaviour. Drinking the tea with only our own thoughts for company he did finally seem to relax and look a little more restored. It was just as well I thought as we needed to get the herd in for milking. However much I had learned doing the main jobs alone was not something I was entirely comfortable with.

Charlie finally spoke, he glanced at the clock on the wall and said, "We have about half an hour, we better get the ladies in for milking. Time for me to explain what's been going on."

"You know Adam if you had not been there today I would have been in a lot of trouble, at best would have been cattle all over the place damaging John's potato crop and me desperately late to get back here for milking."

"Well, all's well that ends well," was all I could think to say. I had no wish to prevent him speaking.

"That's as maybe, but I can't carry on like this."

"Have you been to the Police?" I asked him.

"John reckons I should, but what with? What can I tell them? I'm not a lawyer but even I know I would need to have some proof of what they were doing and then I would probably need to go to court to get some sort of injunction. Not only do I not fancy trying to pay for that, assuming I can even afford it, but tell me just how am I supposed to do that and manage this place?"

He had a point of course. I could offer to help, but as we both know me staying here indefinitely was not on so another course was needed. So I simply said, "Why don't you start from the beginning?"

To begin with I thought he was going to avoid telling me as he stood up but he only stood in order to take down a pad of paper and a pencil from what passed as his office, basically the window sill directly behind where he sat, which held all of the cattle's papers, his milk records and a heap of other famr, related paperwork. How it all stayed there was anyone's guess.

With the pad in front of him turned so that it was long ways on he drew three oblong shapes, down across the page, two the same length and one slightly shorter. Above them he drew parallel lines and wrote 'the lane' in between them. To the right of the page as he looked he wrote 'village' and to the left he drew two more parallel lines and wrote coast lane. This lane bisected the lane at the front of the farm house and ran all the way down to the River Severn. The shortest oblong was next to the coastal lane and he wrote 'John's' in the space and in the centre he wrote 'mine' and in the one closest to the village he wrote 'Old Farm'.

Pointing with his pencil he explained that before the First World War all three farms had been part of a much larger estate. During the economic crisis in the 1920's the estate that owned the farm had severe financial difficulties and broken the farm in to several parts to sell off. His grandfather, then a tenant farm worker in what was now Charlie's home, bought the middle strip and John Stone's family acquired the land to the north of Charlies place. Old Farm had been bought by someone Charlie could no longer remember the name of and by the time he was a teenager had ceased to be a farm and

33

in fact like the original estate was broken down into several smaller plots and Old Farm as such was just the old farmhouse and a two acre garden. He shaded in a part of the land marked as Old farm that corresponded in size to the shortfall from Johns farm next door, leaving the westerly part of his own farm separating the two parts.

Pointing at the shaded area he explained the Carters had bought the land unbeknownst to Charlie some years ago.

He said, "I only found out when I tried to buy it or at least rent it as I have been trying to grow the farm. One of the reasons we have land in parcels all over the place is because I have had to buy bits as I have gone along, so the fields we were at today are actually both rented but I have another twenty acres next to them. The original farm my grandfather bought only had about sixty acres which is not remotely economic these days so I have bought about sixty acres of my own over the last thirty years and I rent another forty. I have had a lot of conversations with John about buying his place one day but it was always dependent on what his family want and so far we have not been able to do a deal. Anyway the land between the bottom of Johns place and the river is only partially useful to farm, the bulk of it is water meadow and I never knew who actually owned it. For years John rented some of it for when he ran a few cattle but these days he just grows haylage and some potatoes. It might seem odd that I don't know who John's landlord was but these parcels of land have been broken up and changed hands so often it is near impossible to know, besides they tend to have been run as part of one of the farms for as long as I can remember. Johns tenancy came up for renewal last year and he could not get it renewed. The Carters had bought it. They also applied for and got planning permission to build about 15 new homes on the land to the back of Old Farm, the bit John owns gives them access to the road and of course my land sits in the way of that acccss. They made me a fair offer to buy it but I refused, I actually said I would buy the land to the back of Old farm but they just laughed. They then sent a fancy lawyer from Bristol in to see me with an offer to buy all of my farm."

"Why didn't you take it?" I asked.

His expression was one of anger, he said, "Because I don't want to sell, it's my life here and besides, Gordon one day will take on the farm."

This did not seem to be the best time to point out that his son Gordon was nowhere to be seen and had been gone for several months. Charlie took a long breath before letting his breath exhale and develop into to a sigh, I could not be sure but it looked to me as thought there was moisture in his eyes.

"Ok, I know it does not look great to anyone from the outside, but however it looks to you and anyone else, this is my farm, my family's farm and I have every expectation that my son will take it on." He paused briefly. "And even if he does not I am not about to sell the farm to a bunch of bully property developers, in fact all they make me want is to see to it their scheme fails." His expression had hardened a good deal, so I asked what they had been doing.

It had started with a few simple thefts and minor disturbances. The first being a PTO, or Power Take Off attachment, missing from a tractor, a flat tyre on a muck trailer and a broken water hose to one of the field water drinkers.

"To begin with I thought I had mislaid the PTO and not noticed an issue with the trailer tyre, but things started to go wrong to frequently. I mean stuff goes wrong on a farm, you've seen that but not as frequently as was happening. Then about a week after the first few things happened I got a letter from the Carters, well I say letter it was a hand delivered note, asking me if I might reconsider my attitude to selling and then going on to say as it would be a shame if things kept going wrong on the farm. I ignored it of course but then more serious things started to happen, one of the tanks for the milk in the diary was contaminated and I had to drain all the milk and get the whole thing cleaned and sterilised. I have no idea how they did it but they have simply gone through periods of causing things to go wrong, get stolen or simply moved so I cannot find them. All the time making it very difficult for me to actually run the farm. Each time there was an increase in the number of things happening then the same pattern a few days with nothing going wrong, life seeming to become normal again and then either a letter or a call asking me to sell. They were clever enough never to make any written and direct threats, just implication and suggestion, things like it must be difficult for an old man to manage the farm, imagine what it would be like in a year or two. That sort of thing."

It was hard to know what to say to him, even harder for me to think of any way I could help him. As with any day on the farm I simply had no time to think as the clock had moved inexorably on and it was now time to get on with milking. Without a word between us we both stood and made our way out of the kitchen and headed to bring in the herd. As with most milking times the cows were already moving towards the gate and waiting, it never ceased to be a marvel to me that they knew not only where to head, but made their way helpfully towards the field gate.

We got on with the routine of the job at hand and finished up around the normal time before heading back to the house for something to eat and as usual an early night in bed. Before heading up stairs I told Charlie I would drive over to check the steers first thing and make sure all was well.

The following morning, I was up early and drove round to check on the cattle in Charlie's beaten up Toyota pickup. Fortunately all was well with the steers and no additional problems seemed to have arisen. On the way back to the farm I collected the electric fencing and the battery pack. They were needed in the new field as the steers would only be there for a couple of days before they were taken to market. It seemed to me that the day which had started with bright sunlight and was already quite warm was going to be a good day. I could not have been more wrong.

Whatever caused me to walk into the kitchen at the moment Charlie opened the package that arrived that morning I will never know. What I do know is the horror on his face was terrifying. A mask of death. I had never seen a man look so incredibly horrified. Not being one of life's most eloquent people I was at least remotely sensitive, so I said nothing. In fact I did nothing, for a moment at least. Charlie was holding a small letter sized envelope in his right hand, in his left he had whatever it was he had taken from the envelope. To my eyes it looked like a letter but something made it bend at the top, as if weighted somehow. I might not be the best educated guy on earth but even I knew letter writing paper tended not to have weighted edges. I must have been at the kitchen door several minutes before Charlie even knew I was there. He glanced up briefly, his head bowing down like a beaten man before he lifted it slowly and stared at me. The terror still in his eyes. Shock like that could kill a weaker man. He fixed his eyes on me briefly before stretching his left hand to me, offering the letter. Taking it from his outstretched hands at first I held his look. Maybe due to looking at him I did not register the weight of the paper. It was only as I attempted to raise it to read that I noticed the top of the paper flop over and that I fully registered the unnatural weight. I looked down to read and had to grasp the top of the paper rather than being able to hold the page at its edge. When I straightened it I saw what was causing the paper to bend so much. Taped to the top left edge of the paper was a bullet, the whole thing, shell case and the business end. Beneath it in thick black text were written the words, "Time to decide old man."

As threats went this one was fairly compelling, to me the obvious course of action was to involve the Police. However Charlie managed to persuade me that would be a waste of time. The local bobby was not a fan of Charlie's and the nearest proper police station was a good ten miles away and Charlie was convinced that the Carter's clever legal team would manage to prevent anything being taken seriously. Added to which he said how the hell was the farm to be run, if he put the time into dealing with the Carters the farm would come to a halt and they would have won anyway. On this at least he had a point.

I did the only thing I could think of and put the kettle on to make tea. What else do the English do in times of crisis? It was whilst staring out of the window waiting for the kettle to boil that the germ of an idea came to me.

"Charlie, where do the Carters live?"

He looked at me as though I was an idiot, maybe I was with what was in my mind.

"They own the property that overlooks the river but I don't think they live in there. In fact I am not sure where their home is if that's what you mean, but they have one of those mobile home type things on the land in front of the house. One of the family lives in it. Why do you need to know?"

"I just had an idea that might get your problem resolved for good."

One of the few good things I had ever done in my life, an achievement if you like, was to save the life of a young boy. His name was Ashley Prentice, he was now a teenager, but when I was in my teens he had been a four year old; he'd managed to wander out of his mother's sight not far from home and fallen into an open cesspool. That I was close by was for him a lucky break and for me as usual a sign I was doing something I shouldn't have been. That bit is best left to another time. What is critical though is Ashley's father became my friend for life. A decent generous and truly amazing man, Dave Prentice was also not someone you messed with. At the time of Ashley's accident his father was stationed in Basra Iraq. Sergeant Major David Prentice MC was not only a war hero but an expert marksman. Twice a winner of the Queens Medal at Bisley and one of the British Army's best shots. Strictly speaking I was referring to former Sergeant Major Prentice but his retirement certainly did not disqualify him from my plan.

Not only did Dave think he owed me forever, but I knew for a fact that he had although not legally, access to the type of weapon needed to fire the bullet I was now looking at. As I said before I am no expert with guns but Dave had taken me both clay pigeon and pheasant shooting. He had given me a few lessons in the use of a shotgun and most importantly for my idea to work he had shown me his gun collection. I was confident but not certain of my gun facts but I was completely sure that Dave Prentice was not only the man for my plan, but more importantly the kind of man more than happy to carry that plan out.

When I tracked him down Dave was only too happy to help. He promised to be with me the following day.

As a former special forces sniper Dave had no need for my help in getting himself organised. What he did need was me to show him on the map where the Carter's home was and to guide him across Charlie Ashton's land to a point where he could see the place. After that I left him to it. He told me he would make his own way back to the farm when his task was complete. With that I left him to it.

I had no idea how long Dave would be and I had decided not to explain my plan to Charlie, indeed he was completely unaware of Dave's presence. I assumed that he put my comments of the day before down to bravado on my part and an urge to help him. In turn he naturally assumed the plan I had was either unworkable or imagined. Either way without much said between us we got on with the day's work.

For me the day passed both quickly and enjoyably, yet another bright summer's day, the cattle all behaved themselves and aside from the need to shift a few bales of straw using the tractor there were no extra jobs.

Charlie and I had just come in from milking when there was a knock on the door. Charlie rose to answer but I beat him to it, after all he had no idea who Dave Prentice was. It did briefly cross my mind that it might not be him but the thought was only brief and was soon despatched the way of all unwanted things. I could tell from the size and shape of the shadow through the frosted glass in the door that it was indeed Dave Prentice. I wasn't entirely clear how things would play out and I certainly had not quite fathomed how to explain to Charlie who Dave was and what he was doing at the farm. I had half an idea and that was it. Fortunately Dave was not carrying anything with him. No gun and no other implements that he might have used. I assumed he had done as I suggested and left the large bag he had been carrying inside the dairy. I had no doubt he had probably been around and watched us finish up the cattle waiting until we had done before he quietly made his way to the dairy and stowed his bag. Now I needed to introduce him to Charlie.

I took the simple way out, eloquence not being my strong suit.

"Charlie, this is Dave Prentice, he's a friend of mine and has come down to help sort the problem with the Carters," I said.

Charlie looked a little perplexed. I could see him trying to figure how this large man in his late forties was going to help sort his issues with the Carters out. Whatever went through his mind he did at least afford him a better greeting than when he met me for the first time. But then again Dave had not just stumbled out of his barn at dawn.

"Good to meet you Dave," he said extending his hand, "Charlie, Charlie Ashton." He stepped aside and indicated the kitchen table. "Come in, we are just about to have some tea, would you like some?" They say manners maketh the man and in Charlie's case old habits do die hard.

"Good to meet you too Charlie and yes a cup of tea would be just grand. I'm parched," Dave replied.

I bet he was, I have no idea exactly where he had been for the last ten hours but I knew for sure tea making facilities were not available.

With a welcome guest in his house auto pilot kicked in for Charlie and fortunately for me it meant he had his mind on other things and could not come up with many questions. He did enquire as to how he had got to the farm. Charlie might be ageing but his hearing was on a par with the average bat and he certainly had not heard a vehicle. As a former NCO Dave Prentice was adept at providing answers to awkward questions and he went directly into professional mode.

"I'm parked up the lane close to village." Which I guessed was probably true. "I couldn't work out which property was yours so I walked."

"Oh, right, I see," Charlie said, turning to the kettle and his teapot. I still found his tea making ritual a little unreal but it was the same every time and always had his full concentration. It was only as he put the pot on the table that he spoke again. "Do you want to bring it down here now you know where we are?"

"Yes, that would be good. But let's have this tea first if that's ok," he said, "and then we can maybe talk about this little difficulty you have."

"Right, yes, right oh," Charlie responded and he stood to pour us each a mug of tea. Dave's sergeants mess technique went into overdrive asking Charlie all about the farm the animals and what life was like in this part of Gloucestershire. He did a remarkable job in distracting Charlie. He was also concerning me as I was beginning to wonder if his diversionary conversation were to cover up for a failed mission.

45

I was beginning to get seriously worried about what was going on when the telephone rang. The ring seemed so incredibly loud in the kitchen I don't think I had ever been in the kitchen when it went off. On the rare occasion I had heard it ring I had been in the dairy and now knew why we could hear over there, the external bell was just outside the kitchen door and went off like an air raid siren.

Charlie rose and answered the phone which was a wall mounted affair just inside the door. It was reachable to answer from outside without the need to take dirty boots off to get to it. He answered it with his usual monosyllabic tone and then didn't say a word, just listened. His face went through a myriad of expressions; surprise, disbelief, suspicion and then finally a small smile of pleasure as he hung up. For once Charlie Ashton was a little lost for words. He walked back to the table and sat down. He stared briefly into his mug of tea before looking up at my somewhat expectant face.

"That was Carter on the phone, he told me they are withdrawing the offer for the land and the farm. Apparently they have had a change of heart about developing the land at the back and want to sell. He said his lawyer would be here in the morning with written confirmation and a proposal for me to farm the land at the back of Old Farm whilst I consider whether to buy or not. Six months rent free."

He rubbed his face double handed the way I had seen him do it many times in recent weeks. He sighed one of his standard sighs. "I can't believe it," he said.

"Well that's good news," Dave said. "Maybe my trip was not needed after all"

I sipped my tea still unsure if this was an unexpected turn of events or if Dave's actions had produced such a rapid response. Joining in the diversionary aspect of the discussion, "Shall we wait until tomorrow before we decide anything. Maybe Dave can stay the night?" I looked at Charlie as I asked and he replied in the affirmative.

The following day Charlie and I went about the normal morning routine and Dave came along to help with a bit of lifting. We got back to the house for some breakfast at just after nine o'clock and at precisely 9.30am a car drew up outside and a smartly dressed woman in her early forties stepped out of the car. She reached into the back seat and produced a slim briefcase and headed to the kitchen door. Introducing herself as the Carters solicitor she asked if she could speak to Mr Ashton in private. So I suggested that Dave might like to come with me to check on the steers.

As soon as we were in the Toyota I asked him what he had done.

After I had left him Dave had spent a little bit of time familiarising himself with the lay of the land and had even scouted round the mobile home and the empty farm house. The place it seems was empty. He identified a few items of interest and then had gone back to the bottom of the field where I had left him and he found himself the ideal spot to wait.

He was holed up for another hour before a shiny new Ford pickup arrived, clearly it had not been used on a farm. The driver had reversed the vehicle into the drive and parked by the mobile home before getting out and going into the home.

With the sound suppressor attached to his rifle Dave had then shot out the front tyre on the driver's side. He then waited, he was beginning to worry that his plan might fail as he had to wait a further two hours before the man reappeared and went to get into the pickup. As he got to the driver's door he noticed the flat tyre and moved to the front of the vehicle. As he stood hands on hips staring at the tyre Dave shot out the tyre on the other side. The man jumped at the sound of escaping air and looked at the tyre in disbclief.

After a few moments of thought the man went back into the mobile home and came back out dressed in work clothes this time. He went to the back of the pickup and recovered a jack. Dave said he had wondered if the guy could possibly have two spares. The guy then went back to the rear of the truck and dragged a spare out wheeling it neatly to the front of the vehicle before laying it down handily for him to retrieve before returning to the jack. At this point Dave then put a round in the spare tyre. This time the guy panicked. What he thought was happening heavens only knew Dave said, but one thing he probably had not figured was that someone had shot out all three tyres. At first he ran around the car looking every which way before darting back inside the mobile home.

Dave had been quick to his feet and got to the vehicle without being seen and left the envelope he and I had prepared on the front step of the mobile home. He retraced his steps and once again took up his vigil. A further twenty minutes passed and the guy came out of the door and immediately saw the envelope. Apparently he just stared at it to begin with and then looked around as if to see who had put it there before picking up. Dave said he wished he could have videoed what happened next to show me and Charlie.

The man, Dave reckoned was in his early thirties so clearly not the head of the family, opened the envelope and for a moment nothing happened. The he looked like he had a case of St. Vitus dance, dropped the envelope and ran back inside the mobile home. By now Dave was laughing almost uncontrollably and I was grinning like a Cheshire cat. We had written a very short note for the recipient. Stuck to the note was an empty shell case. The note said, "Decision made... over to you."

By the time Dave and I got back to the farm the solicitor was just getting back into her car. We waited for her to leave before going into the kitchen. Charlie was sitting at the table with the letter the lawyer had given him in his hand. He looked up as we walked in.

"I've read this over three times, I still can't understand and I am concerned this is all some sort of dream," he said. I glanced at Dave with a suppressed smile on my face, his face was inscrutable.

"I'm sure everything is just fine Charlie," I said. "There is no way that letter is fake, don't worry."

With his face looking years younger Charlie looked at Dave and said, "I'm sorry you seem to have had a wasted trip, no need for whatever plan you had now."

Staying in the doorway, Dave replied, "Looks like you're right Charlie, I'll take my leave then." With that he turned and walked out of the kitchen.

Eugene Clayton's Lucky Break

I woke with a jolt, my brain and head momentarily separated; the sensation was awful. A feeling of liquid spreading around my head and moving on down my neck, as though an artery had split and my mind was losing quarts of blood.

As my eyes focused, I realised I hadn't suffered a brain bleed. The sleep from which I was waking was deep, born of exhaustion. Slowly I began to recognise my surroundings the ache in my limbs started to remind me of what lead to the exhaustion. I felt a sudden pain in my right hand, as my mind focused on it the pain intensified. It started to throb.

Raising my head took a huge amount of effort; the pain threatening to split it in two. The pain in my right knee announced itself, urgent, demanding, clearly far worse than my hand or head. It had my attention.

Different parts of my body were competing for attention. '*I'm in a worse state*', they screamed. The fact of the matter was I felt like I had been hit by a truck and somehow walked away, simply every part of me hurt, the right side worse than the left.

Somehow I lifted my head, blinked my eyes and looked down at my right hand. It was covered in blood. My heart jolted in panic, suddenly racing as my next immediate thought was that I was dying. How ironic if it were true that my own heart should seek to accelerate the end.

I stared for a few seconds before remembering it was not my blood covering my hand. Looking more carefully I could see it was not just my hands, but my whole being, I had been soaked in blood, like I had taken a bath in an abattoir. The pain in my head intensified, as my mind awoke so the memory of how I came to be coated in blood started to return.

Saturday night had begun like any other; I had come in from feeding the chickens, hogs and tending the chores around the farm. I was worn out, tired and in need of food. But like any other night of the week there was little around to satisfy my hunger and even if the opposite were true I had no capacity or desire to prepare food.

Since my father's death eating had always been a challenge, not that he had been a superstar chef, but he could at least make a simple meal that was edible. I couldn't boil eggs without burning the water. Farming hogs and basic cookery were the only skills my father possessed; his abilities with people had driven my mother into the arms of another man when I was only seven years old. As well as the good sense to leave the old man, she and her new beau had moved off to Australia; I hadn't heard from her in thirty years. From leaving school to my father's death when I was aged 27 the only remarkable thing that happened in my life was that I had not killed him before the cancer took him. The only exceptional thing in my life was my loyalty to that same man.

With little to eat and no inclination to learn to cook that night, the same as countless times before, I showered and pulled on a clean shirt and fresh pants. I made sure Boris was fed and watered before heading out.

Boris was a cross breed dog I had picked up as a stray, it's hard to say what breed he was, he was as tall as an Irish Wolfhound, his coat resembled a retriever and his temperament was more like that of a spaniel. He owed his name to a brief flirtation I had had with tennis, in particular to a half-crazy German guy who beat all comers when I was watching on TV. Whatever he was, I had no idea where he had come from and he was as loyal as could be. On my way to the door I patted him on the head and picked up my rifle from the rack. I could never know if a fox in search of a cheap meal might cross my path, besides if I'm honest I enjoyed shooting the critters.

The ageing Chevy truck that served both as farm work horse and personal transport was beginning to look beyond careworn, that it still functioned was a miracle. It was not a new vehicle when I purchased it from the agricultural store out near the interstate a couple of years before my father's death. I had never been in a new truck let alone bought one, but maybe a replacement was needed. The driver's door didn't so much open as drop sideways on its hinges to my touch, the keys already in the ignition and my Remington over and under in the clips next to the stick shift. There was no reason to remove either as crime in Grayson County was as common as beer at the local pastor's meeting hall.

Despite its age the old truck fired up first time, the heavy Detroit lump rumbling like some sort of has been NASCAR racer.

The six mile drive over to Harry's Chicken and Rib Shack took twenty minutes down the tortuous dirt track that passed for a road, only the last half-mile being paved as the track gave way to the road into Grayson.

To the best of my knowledge if you didn't eat bacon, chicken, eggs, pork or ribs you would have to leave the county. Probably the state for all I was aware. I had been out of the state once, briefly, when a school teacher encouraged me to think about college. I went with him to Louisville, Kentucky to see what college life might be like along with a few others from my high school. Even there the only meal I had eaten was chicken and fries. What else would you eat?

The teacher was a well-meaning New Yorker who had an early missionary like zeal for bringing education to smaller town communities. His time at Grayson High cured him and last I heard he had moved back to the city.

Fortunately Harry could serve chicken and slaw with fries quicker than the drive over. I had no idea whether it was better than elsewhere or not, I had only eaten chicken somewhere else once before. I did know his sauce was better than the passable imitation my father could throw together, but that was it. As usual I washed the whole lot down with a root beer before a large helping of apple pie and ice cream followed by coffee. It wasn't late when I left, there were more diners arriving than leaving, I barely said a word to a soul the whole time I was there.

Revived by the food I drove into Grayson with the thought of stopping by the local country music bar for a beer. Sometimes they had live music on, provided by a wannabe local group trying to get some worthwhile practice in or occasionally a struggling band moving down the music world in the opposite direction. Grayson was only somewhere folk went through, few stopped and when they did it was a short stay.

It was only a ten minute ride into Grayson from Harry's place, the town grandly sporting a sign announcing the town limits and population of 1,250. Based on what I saw I'm sure that was an exaggeration. As I moved on to Main Street I could see several cars pulled into the side of the road on both sides where once horses would have been tied to hitching rails.

Grayson's one and only bar was about a third of the way down Main Street on my left as I drove. Courtesy of the lousy headlights on my truck it was only when I drew closer that I recognised Sheriff Barnwell's Crown Victoria pulled up outside. I took my foot off the brake and pressed down on the gas. I was not high on Sheriff Barnwell's list of most popular people; he had held my father in the same high regard, our two families having feuded for as long as anyone could remember. To make things worse the Sherriff's son Chase Barnwell had been a contemporary of mine at school; he seemed to hate me more than anyone as I refused to rise to his baiting.

My lack of desire to join in the mutual hatred upset my father more than the Barnwells. Before he got sick there was nothing he seemed to enjoy more than the latest ruck with someone in the Barnwell family.

It's not that I'm soft or anything, but fighting folk just because that's what you do never seemed a good enough reason to me. The one time I had come to blows with Chase Barnwell came after he hurled a baseball at my back during a game at school. Since I had never reacted before he probably figured it was safe and would draw a few laughs from those who always seemed to be drawn to him, more for fear of his bullying behaviour and size than for liking his company. Why I reacted as I did I've long forgotten, but the game was going badly; in theory we were on the same side playing a high school from the next county. The ball hit me in the left shoulder as I walked back to second base. It stung like hell. Somehow I avoided raging, I bent and picked up the ball, tossed it to the pitcher, marched up to Chase and laid him out with a single right hand upper cut.

Working with hogs, fighting off my father and cutting wood was as good a way as any of building strength. Anyone in Grayson County knew. Aside from the stunned silence and the cancellation of the game that's the only time I was in serious trouble at school, but Chase Barnwell had stayed away from me from that day, sadly though it had not eased his hatred of me.

I turned the pickup around at the far end of the street and headed out of town. It was just before the turning for the southern track home that I saw the car half off the road to my left, there was only one stop light working and a turning indicator flashing as if the driver had intended to pull back onto the road. If the old Chevy's lights had been any good I would probably have seen the body lying in the road next to the car much sooner than I did.

Seeing the car late I hit the brakes hard; so hard I was flung forward in the seat, I hit the steering wheel with my chest, my head bounced forward with whiplash, as I did my hands slipped off the steering wheel, my right arm went between the spokes, twisting my wrist as the wheel jerked whilst the truck came to a stop. Wearing seat belts wasn't something anyone in Grayson bothered with. Chances are mine wouldn't have worked in any case.

I had stopped the truck dead in the middle of the road; I jumped out, adrenalin overpowering any discomfort I felt from colliding with the steering wheel.

As I approached the body I could see what I assumed to be a pool of blood spread wide on the road. I couldn't

59

get close without treading in it, I hardly needed to get close, as it was obvious what I now know to be a man was dead. Half his head was missing and he had a cavernous wound just below his chest.

There was no question he had been shot at least twice, probably with a heavy calibre weapon. I had seen horrid wounds before but only on animals, never a human. I stepped back, recoiled and almost threw up on the spot. Instead I nearly wet myself as a terrified voice called out from beyond the car. The voice was coming from the ditch. The voice sounded hushed almost as though its owner wanted to remain undetected. I ducked to the back of the vehicle and looked down into the ditch.

"In here" was all I heard, the light was poor and my eyesight struggled to adjust to the dark but I could see someone lying in the ditch.

"Get down, in here, they are still out there," said the voice. I ducked down and joined the mystery voice. The guy who belonged to the voice was about my age, slender and around six feet tall. What I could see of his face was covered in cuts, blood smeared all over his head and around his shirt collar. All I managed to understand from him was they had been driving along the road when they saw someone standing in the road, they slowed only to see the stranger in the road raise his arm and fire several shots at the vehicle none of which hit him or his passenger but the windscreen shattered they lost lights and he had slewed off the road. Without thinking both occupants had jumped out of the car he was fortunate the ditch was handy as when he had left the car more shots rang out, hitting his friend. So far that was it.

I could not extract anything further. But it did not take much to realise whoever had fired at the car and killed the man now lying in the road was still around and probably deciding how best to finish what had been started. Right on cue a voice called out from behind.

"Stay exactly where you are and don't look round. I can shoot you both with ease."

I stared straight ahead, nothing in my life had prepared me for this, and I had no idea what to do. My body started to shake with fear; sweat broke out on my forehead at odds with how cold I suddenly felt. I had two loaded weapons in my truck, why had I not taken one out when I saw the car pulled over? Then again why the hell would I? Shoot outs happened on TV, not in Grayson County, besides, I had only shot animals before, never people.

I heard muffled voices behind us so there was clearly more than one person back there. Then I heard the passenger door of my truck being pulled, it was so worn it made a sound like an old field gate. Moments later footsteps came towards us, a different voice this time, a woman's voice, it came as a shock.

"Stranger, if you want to live you move to your right away from that asshole, do you hear me?"

I opened my mouth to answer, but could only manage a strange croak.

"I said, do you hear me?"

As neither my mouth, or voice would function for an answer I shuffled away to my right leaving a couple of feet between us.

"That's better. Both of you stay exactly where you are, I will not hesitate to shoot."

The voice behind me called out to whoever else was with her but I could not see who or where the other person was. I could hear car doors being opened and what I guessed was the trunk of a car. There was silence for several minutes and then I heard footsteps behind and a hushed conversation.

The same voice spoke again. "There are now two guns pointing at you, I am going to move to your left, the other gun is directly behind you."

A second voice, this time a man joined in, "And I can't miss from here." I heard the man moving and glanced to my left to see him appear in my peripheral vision. His gun was pointed directly at the man next to me.

Holding his gun steady and shining a bright torch he spoke directly to the guy in the ditch.

"Now you piece of shit, tell me where the bag is."

"I don't know what you're talking about," my neighbour in the ditch replied, his voice lacking strength and breaking as he spoke.

"The bag you stole asshole. Don't play the dumb cluck with me, we both know what you and your recently departed brother took from us, so if you want to live just tell me where you put it."

"I don't have any bag."

"Listen dickhead, we are not stupid, it did not take long to find out what a pair of low-life thieves you and your brother are, the only minor challenge was tracking you across the state. I bet you couldn't believe your luck when you found a bag full of cash when you turned our place over, could you? Now I am only going to ask once more before I start shooting lumps off you, where is the bag?"

"Fuck you," the guy replied.

I guess I hadn't expected the man with the gun to fire either so I jumped in terror when he fired the gun. I couldn't see what it was but the report made it sound heavy, that said the guy's scream was louder. I looked over but couldn't see where he had hit him, but my guess was the ankle or foot. The scream turned into steady series of groans and grunts, his breathing was ragged and forced, it reminded me of the reaction a young child has to a bad graze on the knee, I could hear him trying to mask the sound he was making but the pain was clearly too much for him.

"Let's, try again, shall we?" the voice behind the light said. "Now where's the bag, or would you prefer I shoot you in the other foot, or the knee perhaps?"

"No, not again, I'll tell you, just don't shoot me," the guy pleaded, his voice again beginning to crack.

"I'm listening."

"We did take the bag. There was nothing else in your place to take. We were about to take off empty handed, when Bobby decided he need to take a leak. That's where he saw the bag. He figured the closet was a strange place to leave a bag so he opened it. We couldn't believe it so we just took off. We figured staying in the area was dumb as someone with that kind of money stashed was going to come looking."

"Well you were damn right on that one," said the voice behind the light. "Just a pity your solitary brain cell didn't convince you to leave it and get out, woulda saved a heap of trouble for us not to mention you and your brother. So where is it now?"

The terror in the voice next to me seemed to get worse. "Like I said before, we don't got it."

"So where the fuck is it, or do you think I'm an idiot?"

The guy seemed to hesitate I heard the huge intake of breath before he said "We lost it…" his voice trailing off as he spoke.

"Lost it? Where?"

"We got rousted in a card game, some guys took it from us," he said. "We were looking to buy some drugs and the guy we was speaking to invited us to join him and some buddies of his for a little late night game a stud. Bobby was pretty good with the cards so we figured we could maybe turn a profit."

"Don't you go fucking with me," the voice behind the light said.

The woman behind me interrupted before anyone else could speak, "I think maybe he is telling the truth."

"Shit, so what happened then?" the guy with the torch continued.

"Bobby was doing ok to begin with, but then suddenly he started losing. But he was losing stupid and I could tell from his face something was wrong. He was getting more and more pissed as he started to lose more. After the last hand he lost, he stood and said he was quitting. But the big guy across from him said why, he had plenty of dough he could most probably win back what he'd lost. Bobby looked at him and said he don't play with no cheats."

"So your Bobby really is, sorry *was* stupid then. Accusing strangers in a strange place of cheating at cards is not a good way to gain respect. But none of this is helping me get my money back and I am getting bored of standing here, so where did the money go?"

The guy next to me was breathing easier, but the fear was still in his voice and the pain in his ankle was causing him to moan before drawing in a large breath as he continued, "The big guy never said anything to Bob, he simply stood and pulled a gun on him, two of the others joined in. We figured they had it planned all night. So they simply took the bag and lead us outside.

Told us to get in our car and drive away or stay put and get shot. Weren't nobody going to find us out where we were. So we just did what they said"

"Where was this?"

"I don't know exactly, we stopped in a truck stop just off the I-75 just north of Williamsburg. That's where we spoke to the guy about some dope to smoke. We followed him for about a half an hour into the National Park. He took us to small farm. That's where we got the dope and then the invite to the card game. I ain't no idea where that was, we just followed the farmer in his pickup, we went further into the park. By the time we got to the place it was so dark we couldn't see a damn thing. We only just got out of there before the gas ran dry."

"So who was the guy you asked about the drugs?"

"He worked tables at the truck stop," the guy in the ditch went on to describe him. When he'd finished I obviously couldn't see but I sensed him relax, he probably closed his eyes. I did to as I had no idea what was going to happen next. I did not need to wait long. The guy with the torch fired four shots into the man next to me, bits of him flew all over, his blood splashing my face even though I was a good few feet from him.

With the sound of the last round still audible the voice behind the torch spoke. Clearly to me. "Mister we got no truck with you. We are going to leave here now and you are best advised to stay exactly where you are. I suggest at least for an hour. If you have any issues with that I will not hesitate to let you join the piece of shit I already shot. Understood?"

I croaked a yes in answer to him.

"Good," he said. "One more thing, best you develop a fast case of amnesia about tonight, cause I know where to come looking if any of this gets out," he added before turning away. The light moved away from me and I just stared into the distance.

I heard the muffled voices of two people speaking, then I heard two metallic sounds, like something being struck with a hammer. A moment later I heard two gunshots separated by a few seconds. Then silence.

I have no idea how long I stayed in the ditch. For what seemed an eternity I didn't move at all, I never even glanced at the man beside me. By the time I did my eyes had adjusted well to the nightlight so maybe it was about twenty minutes. I looked to my left, the man was still, I could not make anything out of him other than a dark shape, like a smooth rock. I listened carefully but could hear nothing so I moved towards him turning as I did, reaching out my right hand to check for a pulse. I can only describe what I touched as feeling like mush and goo. This time I did vomit, I threw up all over the corpse and my own trousers. I scrambled to get away. As I tried to get traction up out of the ditch I slid then fell back in landing half on the dead man, my horror quickly turning to panic moving as fast as I could to my left to escape the ditch.

Somehow I pulled myself out of the ditch, I lay for a second on the roadside in a bid to control my panicked breathing. As my breathing subsided, the adrenalin reduced, I began to feel the pain in my right hand and wrist, my neck hurt like hell and every muscle in my legs was aching. I realised as well as hurting myself when the truck stopped I must have been tensing every muscle in my body whilst lying in the ditch, now as I a little more relaxed I felt like I had hiked across the Daniel Boone National Forest carrying a fifty pound pack.

When I approached my truck, taking care to walk well away from the dead guys car I noticed the front seemed lower. That was when I realised what the gunshots were, both front tires were flat. I opened the driver's door and saw my CB radio had taken a beating too as it hung from its rack, clearly unusable. I didn't have a cell phone, in any case signals out here were about as reliable as the US Postal service. I was surprised to see my shotgun still stowed in the rack: I reached down to my left, the rifle was also still in the vehicle. I guess they figured a shotgun was no threat and they had probably not even noticed the rifle.

I sat in the driver's seat for some time thinking nothing and feeling little else, my mind seemed numb. Maybe it was shock, I have no idea, but for a period at least the ache in my body seemed to be kept at bay along with any conscious thought. As my head began to come to I figured I needed to move on, what I couldn't fathom was where or how. The citizen part of me realised I had somehow to tell the Sherriff, but the very thought made me shudder. Knowing Sherriff Barnwell he'd probably lock me up and have me stand trial for the murder of two men. Believe me when I say he would have found a way to fit me with the crime. Besides it was six mile trek back to town and I did not feel like the walk. Then again I hardly fancied the walk home.

My mind retreated back to wherever the hell it had gone the last time. I stared directly ahead, not really noticing the body in the road to my left, it was only then I realised I had not heard another vehicle when the two killers had left me. As my brain started to come back to itself I decided the best thing was to take off and hope no one put me and the events of the night together.

I started the truck, which at least was straightforward. Driving it was not. The ride home was slow and tortuous with the front wheels feeling like they would fall off at every small bump in the road. Steering was as difficult as anything I had ever tried, the power steering was lousy to begin with, but with two flat tires and the weight of one of Detroit's ancient V8s resting in front it was like moving the Atlas stones to shift the steering a few inches. I have no idea how long it took to get home, but the sun was rising and the world waking before I got myself stopped outside the cabin.

***

Once fully awake I stripped my clothes off; the blood on my trousers was so thick it had not fully dried. I took a long shower using all the hot water in the process. It was only after I had towelled myself dry and got dressed that I paid any attention to the time, it was early afternoon. I'd been out longer than I realised, I had not fed and watered the animals. Lifting feed with my weakened right arm was not going to be much fun.

For a time at least my mind was so occupied with the animals that I did not give any thought to the events of the night before and what if anything I should do. The first thing was to assess the damage to the truck. Somehow I had to get it operating, either that or the feed for the hogs and chickens would have to be delivered and that cost a fortune.

Whilst I had a serviceable jack and the tools to change the wheels I had only one spare and assuming I had not destroyed the rims on the front wheels I still did not fancy the drive to town to get the truck fixed. I could take the tractor into town but that would take half the day. I decided to deal with it tomorrow and for once sort something to eat for myself, if you can call taking a TV dinner out of the freezer and using a microwave sorting something to eat.

The rest of the day passed without incident, pretty much like hundreds before it, indeed so did the day after. With the passing of nearly 72 hours my body was beginning to ache less and although the shooting was fresh in my mind the worry had strangely abated.

By late morning on the fourth day I was working on how to sort the truck, if for no other reason than the need for animal feed and I was getting tired of microwave food.

The layout of the place was fairly conventional, as the track up crested the small rise from the creek below it opened out into a fairly large area, big enough to park a dozen vehicles without any problems; the house was set almost side on to the open space. On the right as you came up were the farm sheds in a line that ran up to the house, the smallest shed which doubled as a garage was closest to the house. It was the only one without a door, the double doors long since ceasing to work properly, since they served little purpose I had taken them down a couple of years earlier and left the building open. I had the truck in there raised on a jack. I had decided to put the spare on one side and then prop the other, before taking what was left of the tires off the rims so I could take them into the auto shop in Grayson for new tires to be fitted.

I had called an old family friend, at least he was of mine, I can't say what he made of my father, not many thought highly of him.

Pete had been a great help since my father died. He lived about 20 miles north just off the old highway that had been replaced as the main route south by the interstate. The highway bypassed Grayson with a small road running from it north to south, this was the only route into and out of town. The tracks to my place met this road to the north almost where the small road and the highway met and around five miles north of the town to the south.

When I called Pete he was due to go into Grayson to run some errands a day later but was happy to come in earlier and meet me on the northern track, this was not only the easiest place for me to leave the tractor, but the closest route to Harry's for the lunch I had promised Pete for his troubles.

Pete Gill was probably in his late seventies, he had been in Grayson as long as I could remember, he was originally from Pittsburgh. He had joined the army straight from high school, to see the world. Most of what he saw was Vietnam. When he left the military he joined the US Forestry Service and trained as a Forest Ranger. He decided to quit long before his normal retirement age and had moved south to start a smallholding. Old Pete had forgotten more about hogs than I was ever likely to know.

By the time I got to the paved part of the road, Pete was pulled into the side waiting. We exchanged greetings and little else. Pete didn't once ask how come I had two wheels missing tires, but then he wasn't a nosy guy.

We drove into town in near silence. As we arrived at the auto store it struck me as a bit weird that Pete hadn't said a word about events of a few nights earlier. Surely he would have heard something about it?

Pete left me at the auto store and went about whatever business he had in town. The guys in the store got my new tires fixed on pretty quick; I paid cash whilst wincing at the cost.

I sat at the roadside waiting for Pete to return and started to think about how neither Pete nor the guys in the store seemed to know anything about the previous Saturday night. I couldn't come up with a single semi-sensible theory. I was still half expecting a visit from Sheriff Barnwell.

Not talking about it was worse than having to keep my mouth shut. I had no idea how likely or otherwise it was that the two killers would come back. After a wait of about a half hour Pete rolled back up with his truck and we lifted the newly-repaired wheels into the back and set off for the diner. On the drive back out of town up to Harry's Pete started telling me the news he had just gathered in the general store, a fresh drama had arisen in a neighbouring town, the younger sister of our local pastor had run off with a married teacher. Such was the life of our sleepy community. The tale retold Pete quickly started talking about hogs, the price of pork belly and whether it was likely to be a tough year or not. It took me a heap of effort not to ask him if anyone had mentioned anything happening on Saturday night.

The cost of my ride into town was a large helping of just about everything Harry's had to offer. I could never understand how someone could eat like Pete and stay so damned skinny. We parted back at my tractor with nearly as many words as when we had met earlier.

***

I had not long finished fixing the wheels back on my truck when I thought I heard a vehicle in the distance. My thoughts were confirmed when Boris started hollering like we were about to be invaded. Hardly anyone ever drove up to my place.

My head was aching already from thinking through the bizarre silence about last Saturday without Boris making it worse with his racket echoing in the shed. I shooed Boris out and stepped behind him to see a shiny black SUV making its way carefully up the track. Not only did we not get many visitors, no one in the county possessed anything as new and fancy as the big GMC making its way up the track.

I reached into the truck and took my shotgun out of its rack. No need to check if it was loaded, there was no point in my view in having an unloaded shotgun, even if it was only buckshot. I stayed inside the barn and watched the SUV make its way towards the house. Boris had now taken to standing off, his bark reduced to a menacing growl.

The SUV pulled a left turn in front of the house leaving it facing away from me. The engine had barely stopped when both front doors opened and two guys emerged, both in suits nearly as shiny as their ride. So far there was nothing to suggest either posed a threat but given my recent experience of strangers I was assuming the worst. I only wish I had the rifle, just in case.

I watched as both men approached the house, they knocked on the screen door and called out. Clearly no one answered.

Taking a deep breath, I stepped out of the barn's shadows and took very quick steps towards the house. The two guys were sufficiently deep in conversation they did not notice me for several seconds. When they did I kept walking the gun now raised and pointed directly at them, I needed to be close enough for it to have sufficient impact should using it prove necessary.

As one they both slowly raised their hands from their sides. The older of the two, maybe about my age took a step forward and held his right hand up as though trying to stop a car in the road. He immediately began to speak.

"Mister, we just want to speak to you, besides shooting a Federal officer is not likely to prove life enhancing for you, so could we have the gun down please?"

"Not till I seem some ID," I replied.

"Ok mister, I'm going to reach in my pocket and would rather you don't do anything in haste while I do…. Ok?" With that he reached into his jacket pocket with his right hand and slowly withdrew a wallet, before flicking it open.

I was far enough away I could not really see it and in any case I had never seen an FBI agent's ID so for all I knew it could be fake. I figured the likelihood was the ID was not fake, so I lowered the gun.

"Thank you," the guy with the ID said, I'm Agent James Ralston, this is Agent Robson Simpson," he said inclining his head towards his colleague. "We just want to ask a few questions."

I looked hard into his eyes and decided I could trust them. I broke open the shotgun and hung it over my arm. "Inside?" I asked.

We sat around the kitchen table, the two FBI agents declined my offer of coffee.

"Well, mister can we start by learning your name?"

"Eugene, Eugene Clayton" I replied.

"Well, Eugene, do you often greet folk with a loaded shotgun?" Ralston asked.

"Er no sir, I apologise for that," I said my voice drifting off at the end. "I was just a bit jumpy about strangers and all."

"You got any reason to expect strangers calling?" My heart flipped at Ralston's question. They must know something happened I thought. Although I had done nothing wrong, except not report anything. "Or have you seen any strangers around here lately?"

"No sir, I ain't seen anyone, no one tends to head this way, not even the locals call up here," I replied. It was partly true at least; no one did visit my place, except old Pete maybe a few times a year.

"Ok," Ralston continued "The thing is we are looking for a couple of folk and we have reasons to believe they may well have passed through Grayson."

"They in trouble?" I asked.

"Well I'm afraid we're not at liberty to say much, but we are keen to speak to a man and a woman travelling together." He reached into his inside pocket and produced a small folder from which he slipped a couple of items. He glanced at his colleague briefly who gave an almost imperceptible nod. He turned over what I could now tell were photographs. "Have you ever seen these two?" he asked, pushing two pictures towards me.

It was quite accurate when I answered no, because I had not seen the man and woman the previous Saturday. That did not alter the fact that I was fairly sure the pictures I was looking at must be the same man and woman from that night.

"You're absolutely sure?" Agent Simpson asked. They were the first words he'd uttered since they arrived.

"Yes sir," I paused looking at the picture again, "ain't seen these folk."

Ralston started to get up from the table, gathering the pictures as he did. "Okay Eugene, thank you for your time. If you do see these two I want you to contact us on this number," he said handing me a card, it sounded more like an order.

"One further thing, if you see them be very careful as they are dangerous, we've been on their trail for months, they have a habit of disappearing like ghosts".

***

Despite fears of Déjà vu I decided on the Saturday following the shooting to take myself into Grayson, but only after ribs at Harry's. Since my days rarely allowed for much time away from chores around the farm and the yard going out on Saturday night was the highlight of my week. Something about Harry's ribs seemed to spur me on so most Saturday's I managed to get everything done and fed earlier than any other day of the week. I even afforded myself a shower before pulling on a fresh pair of jeans and my smartest shirt.

I was just getting into my truck when the lights of an approaching car pierced the darkening sky. I stopped half in the truck with the Remington firmly in my hand, I'd been convinced for years I might see a fox to shoot on my drive into or back from Grayson but in all the years I'd been doing it, never once had I had need to use it.

I waited as the lights lifted up and down with the car making its way over the bumps and holes in the track, it looked like something from a fairground ride. As the car became more visible I became even more tense, it was Sheriff Barnwell's Crown Vic. Whilst I had no time for Barnwell I figured greeting him with a gun was not going to get things off to a good start, but even so leaving it on the front seat of the Truck as I stepped away took some doing.

The only time I could recall anyone from the Sherriff's office coming to my place was once when a deputy turned out to question the old man about a set to in Grayson. Problem being it had been Barnwell the old man had hit.

The car came to halt outside the house almost exactly where the Feds GMC had pulled up. For a few moments nothing happened, given the lack of light I wasn't even sure it was Barnwell in the car till he opened the door.

Whether he had been any kind of athlete in the past I wasn't sure but now closer to 60 than 50 and weighing something over 250 pounds he moved with all the grace of beached walrus. I wasn't sure he'd seen me and guess he must have known I wasn't in the house despite Boris making enough noise to wake the neighbours if I had any. As he stood still and looked all round, the light from his car giving some sort of vision. Rather than approach the house he rested his hands on the frame of the car door and called my name.

When I didn't respond he carried on as though he knew I could hear him.

"Look Gene, can you just come out to talk? I know we don't see eye to eye on much, but I'm not here for trouble and you ain't in any bother neither so please just come out cause I need to ask you a couple of things."

My heart was racing as there were two main thoughts in my head. The first, maybe something or someone had become aware of the events of a week ago and second, Barnwell hated me. I took a deep breath, stepped away from my truck and took a couple of steps towards Sheriff Barnwell.

"I'm here," I said, stopping some distance from him. He had to turn to see me and his hands came off the car, I half expected him to pull his side arm, but he didn't. In fact he held his hands high in the air as though I had a gun trained on him. I could almost hear the ghost of my father telling me to shoot him while I had the chance. Instead I got all polite.

"How can I help you Sheriff?" I asked.

"Well first up you could come a little closer so we don't need to holler at each other," he said.

"Don't worry Sheriff" I said only Boris can hear us and he ain't ever gonna tell.

"Who's Boris?"

"My dog Sheriff, that's him making all the noise in the house."

"Oh, ok, I get you" Barnwell continued. "I just want to ask a couple of questions"

"Am I in any trouble?"

"No, nothing like that I just want to know if you seen a couple of folks round here?" This was becoming a becoming a common theme I thought.

"What sort of folk?" I asked. I had no idea where this was going but I was troubled that first the FBI and now the local Sheriff seemed to be looking for people and had stopped by to ask me.

"Well if you'd come a bit closer I could be a bit more candid with you," he responded.

"Like I said Sheriff, ain't no one round here to hear anything we say."

"Ok, look, have you had the FBI round here as it seems they been snooping all round my town asking all sorts a questions to all sorts of folk."

His town! Barnwell sounded like he had been watching too many old Clint Eastwood movies.

Maybe it was deep in the subconscious or maybe the Clayton genes but something told me not to tell him about the Feds visit.

84

"No Sheriff," I replied, "I ain't seen no one for days."

"Ok, ok, that's good," he said, his head bowed a little, his shoulders dropping as though releasing tension from his body.

"Is there something wrong Sheriff?"

"Well, I probably shouldn't be telling you this," he continued, "but it seems we had a bit of trouble near here a week back. Folk going missing and reports of maybe someone getting shot; on top of that as I said the FBI have been round town asking questions about a man and a woman they're looking for." He paused as if thinking whether to continue or not. "Thing is Gene, law enforcement round here is down to me, we don't really want the Feds stompin all around the place do we? Never know where it might lead," he said.

"No sir, I guess not," I replied.

"Gene, I need you to do something for me, I promise it'll change a lot of things and the way we Barnwells think about the Claytons if you do," he paused for effect before continuing, "I really need you to come see me if you get a visit or a call from the Feds. Do you get my meaning Gene?"

"I believe I do Sheriff," I said, although in truth I had no clue whatsoever about what his meaning was. I could take a few guesses, but based on what he'd said I had more chance of predicting the winner of the 2050 Kentucky Derby.

With our brief exchange over Sheriff Barnwell started to climb into his car, it was something of a task. Before he closed the car door he said, "Remember, come see me if anyone, anyone at all comes asking questions."

In answer I waved my hand. He pulled his door closed and fired up the Crown Vic before heading back the way he came.

***

The next few days passed without incident or further visits from Sheriff Barnwell, the Feds or any other law enforcement. Life was pretty much as normal; rise early, tend the animals, feed Boris, then myself, more chores around the place and the occasional visit to Harry's and Grayson.

A few weeks earlier I had arranged for Pete to come over to help me with some fencing. He had a rig for the tractor to drill holes for posts that saved a huge amount of effort. Because of the distance he had taken the rig off the back of his tractor and brought it over in the back of his truck. We had some trouble fitting it onto my old tractor, but once on we drove down to the field where my fencing needed sorting.

I had agreed to rent a large field adjacent to my own down towards the southern end of my place. It was nearly at the end of the track that lead to the Grayson road, close enough to the ditch in which the stranger had been shot to make me shudder as we got closer.

We began work first drilling holes in the line I had marked out some weeks earlier, before we would ram the upright posts into the holes. Some folks not only had a machine to drill the hole, but also drive the posts into the ground. We had to make do with a battered metal ram with two handles that could only be used by two people working together. More than once we were driven to laughter at our inability to remain coordinated. Though by the time we had got halfway along the line of holes the novelty had worn off and the work was beginning to take its toll.

Quite where Pete got the strength and energy I never knew. Conversation was limited as we worked through the day, finally finishing in the late afternoon. Still enough light for us to get back to my place and for Pete to get home and check on his animals. I was so tired another TV dinner from the freezer was all I could manage. I could not remember going to bed.

I was woken by a combination of insistent banging somewhere on the property and Boris making the most enormous racket. Waking was a bit of an exaggeration, I struggled to come to and recognise the noise. A glance at my watch showed it was 11.30pm, I had only managed about an hour and half's sleep. Groggily I staggered out of bed and grabbed a pair of jeans, stumbling as I pulled them on, nearly tumbling over. Had I done I would no doubt have connected with the solid wood dresser that stood next to the door. As it was I managed to get them on and half pulled up as I headed into the hall. The banging on my door continued unabated. I yelled that I was on the way and to stop but to no avail.

As I made my way through the hall towards my front door Boris eased his racket a little, though whether that was down to my presence of having barked himself hoarse I have no idea. Unbolting the front door took some effort, my efforts at coordination resembled that of a drunk.

When eventually I got the door open my already malfunctioning brain was taken aback by my visitor. If prior to opening the door I had been able to take a guess as to who would be there the last person I would have guessed at was Sheriff Barnwell, but there he was as large as life. Though he looked more fearful than I was, in the light from the hall he appeared white, grey even, his eyes seemed to have sunk into his head and his face carried a worried expression.

He spoke without any pleasantries, not that I should be surprised by that, but no introduction at all, he simply blurted out a question.

"Have you seen Chase?"

Why he would think I might was beyond me, Chase Barnwell was probably less likely to visit me at home than the President. Rubbing my face in an effort to regain some semblance of normality also bought me a few seconds to replay the question and make sure I had not misheard or was actually in the middle of a weird dream.

"No," I eventually replied, "I ain't..." my voice trailed off as though it thought I should add something but my brain couldn't or wouldn't join in.

"You're sure?"

"Of course I'm sure, frankly given your family's long-standing view of the Claytons I am struggling to think of why you could believe Chase would come here. He has long made sure he stayed well away from me," I responded, my brain finally beginning to communicate more efficiently with my mouth.

Sherriff Barnwell's shoulders slumped before he added, "No, I guess you're right… silly of me to ask."

As he uttered the last words he turned on his heel and walked back to his car. Still slightly shaken by his presence I watched as the Sheriff's Crown Vic made its way more quickly than could have been comfortable from the inside at least down the track away from my house.

Now fully awake, I walked into my kitchen and retrieved a beer from the fridge. Although I did enjoy a beer I was not actually in the habit of getting out of bed in the middle of the night to drink beer. But life in Grayson was getting weirder by the minute.

I took the beer out to the porch and sat in my father's old rocker to think through the events of the last couple of weeks. I played the events back through my mind and wondered why a whole lot of different folks seemed to be seeking out some other folks and what the possible connection with my place could be.

I had been close to having my head blown off, I'd had the FBI and the Sheriff visit and that was it. Well that's what had happened but as to why I had no idea. I knew that a man and a woman had been desperately searching for missing money, so desperate they had killed for it. The Feds were keen to track down a man and a woman and had warned me they were dangerous and to call the agents if I saw them. This visit was swiftly followed by the Sherriff asking about the Feds and now asking if I had seen his son. As I say things were getting weird.

On top of all this I was beginning to worry about money quite a bit. Whatever else I thought about my father he had managed to keep the farm pretty much afloat financially and whilst I hadn't ruined it I was struggling. I had made a few silly mistakes in the last couple of years which combined with tough markets for pork had meant I had to dip into the one other surprise the old man had left, a small life insurance policy he had taken with an agent of Northwestern Mutual. It wasn't huge but had helped me a lot in the last couple of years. There was about $11,000 remaining, some of which I was using to fund the rent on the new field and I was also going to use some to purchase further livestock. At least my latest idea was something I'd had sense to discuss with Pete and get his advice.

I didn't get to do too much more thinking, it must have been a combination of the beer and my tiredness but I fell right asleep in the chair on the porch. I woke shivering at 3am and managed to drag myself into bed, where once again I was asleep pretty quickly.

***

The following morning after the normal chores I loaded fencing wire and tools in the pickup and lifted old Boris in the front with me and set off to finish the job I had started with Pete.

All that was left to do was stretch the wire between the posts, although I could manage alone it would have been far easier with Pete's help. I got the first few posts completed easily enough but ran in to a little difficulty at the first turn of the fencing line. The field was on a gentle slope for most of its run, but fell sharply the last few yards to a ditch which itself bordered a small, rarely-used road that ran up to the forest. Grayson County was full of ditches. The road was metalled for about two hundred yards from the Grayson road and turned to dirt for the rest of its length. I drove up it once for a mile or so just to see where it went, but once you got into the trees it turned really dark so I had turned round as soon as I found a suitable spot and had never been up the track since. I couldn't even remember when that was.

The trouble with making the turn with the wire was keeping the tension. I had an old ratchet wire tensioner but the ratchets were worn and I needed to hang on to the wire whilst applying the tension tool. Easy on the level ground, but not so on the slope. After several failed efforts which resulted in me falling and sliding on the slope I decided to take a break for a few minutes before I threw the tool away in frustration, not to mention the need to stop my left arm bleeding where I had grazed it badly.

Calling Boris to me, I walked away from the fence across the ditch onto the paved part of the track and turned towards the Grayson road. I tore a small piece of cloth from my shirt and tied it round the small cut on my arm. Probably too tightly but I wanted to stop it bleeding.

I'm not sure what made me do it, but I decided to cut across the triangle formed by the track and the Grayson road towards the track that lead up to my place. The wooded area was quite thick so I had to keep adjusting the line I took to get through. Ever since the shooting I was bemused that no one had raised the matter. Getting to the ditch where the stranger had died would have been a hell of a lot easier if I'd followed the track to the road and then turned left and walked along it, but something made me head the way I had.

It took a few minutes longer to get through than I expected. The effort of fighting my way through the trees took my mind off my arm, either that or I tied the cloth so tight the lower half of my arm would drop off in time. The undergrowth was so thick I almost fell into the ditch beside the road. I slid down into it and climbed out the other side and stopped for a while to double check where I was.

Looking round I could see I was on the Grayson side of the spot where the guy had been shot. So I walked left up the road. It wasn't difficult to find the place where I had stopped. There were clear tyre marks on the road where I had stopped quickly. Maybe I imagined it but I was also sure I could see a dark patch where the body had lain. What I also figured was someone had made an effort to clean the blood off the road.

Stepping over to the ditch one thing that struck me was the number of boot prints I could see both round the top of the ditch and down into it. It was difficult to see much in the ditch, partly because of the light and partly because Boris was busy and intently sniffing around.

"Boris, get out of there," I called, but received just an increase in the pace of tail wagging. I shouted more harshly at him and finally he turned to look. Patting my leg, I said, "Here Boris, come on," with which he trotted a little reluctantly to me.

After making Boris sit on the side I jumped down into the ditch and bent down to look closer. I could see faint prints that I thought were from my own boots, but overlaid by several others. I'm no tracker but I figured there were at least four other sets of prints in the ditch. There was also congealed blood where the guy had been shot and an impression in the dirt where I had half lain and sat.

I climbed back out on the wooded side and looked down into the ditch and wondered just who had been so keen to get rid of the bodies and why nothing had been heard about it anywhere. The killers wouldn't have done it that's for sure. They took off pretty smartly after shooting the guy. I could see no reason for them to come back. The risk that they might have been seen was too great. Nothing in the last few weeks made any sense.

Glancing at my watch I realised I needed to get back to work or there was no chance I would finish today. For a few seconds I considered walking or jogging back around the road but figured I could make it quicker through the trees. I had only gone a yard when I saw something sticking out of the base of a bush on my left.

It was hard to make out exactly what it was but the regularity of the shape marked it out. I stepped closer and realised what I was looking at was the end of some sort of bag. A brown bag, made of a canvas type material. It was not at all clear if the bag had been put there or simply thrown. I heaved it out of the bush, it was surprisingly heavy.

The bag was fastened by a zip which I tugged open before peering inside. When I looked in I had to sit back in surprise. The bag was stuffed with cash, more dollar bills than I had seen in my lifetime. The first roll I got out were fifties. I rummaged around and found everything from ten dollar bills right up to one hundred bucks.

Even an idiot would know what I had unearthed. The realisation of what this bag was brought a sense of panic to me.

"Jeez," I said out loud. For a few moments I just sat and stared at the bag and its contents not knowing what to do. For a while I considered putting it back. Then of taking it into town to Sheriff Barnwell, before realising I should probably hand it in to the FBI. The more I thought though the more I began to consider the likelihood that the FBI were not all that bothered, they were interested in Bonnie and Clyde or whoever the killers were. I knew it was probably wrong to keep it, but then again....

I finally made a decision. I hefted the bag up to my shoulders and made my way through the wood back to my truck. If progress had been surprisingly difficult getting here it was magnified several times carrying the bag. When I got back to my truck I looked at the unfinished fencing, felt my aching shoulder and figured I'd call it quits for the day.

Boris and I both got in the truck and headed back towards home. I'm never sure what it is that causes you to think something is odd or out of place, but as I drove on to my track there was something not quite right. I had no idea what.

As I rounded the turn that gave me the first glimpse of the yard and my home my heart nearly stopped at the sight immediately in front of me. The fancy shiny GMC which brought the Feds the first time was just drawing to a stop in front of my home.

"Shit," I said out loud, "Boris, looks like we got visitors." I eased off the gas and drove slowly towards the waiting SUV. As I got closer the occupants got out in unison, almost choreographed.

I recognised them both immediately, agents Ralston and Simpson. They stood together at the back of the vehicle hands by their sides. Ralston had a slight smile on his face which eased my fears, if only marginally.

Convinced they knew something about the bag in my truck or that somehow I was now a suspect in heavens knew what crime. I seemed to take an age to get out of the truck. I stepped out and Boris bounded out behind me and instantly started yelling at the agents.

"Boris, stop that" I shouted. For once the dog listened and waited for me to walk towards him and the two agents.

"Hi Eugene," Agent Ralston said, raising his hand slightly, his smile widening. "Real sorry to bother you, but we'd just like to ask a couple of questions. Is that okay?"

My throat felt constricted, it was becoming habitual. "Sure," I managed to croak, whilst walking directly towards the house.

I lead the two agents into the kitchen and indicated they could sit.

"Pleased to see you without a gun, Eugene," Simpson said with a hint of sarcasm as he sat down.

As with their first visit they both declined the offer of coffee. I made myself one as they began speaking, more to keep myself busy than any real need of the caffeine.

"Eugene I wanted to check something with you," began Ralston. "We'd like to know if you know Chase Barnwell?"

I glanced across from the coffee machine, the question coming as a real surprise.

"Sure," I replied keeping the tension out of my voice took some effort. "Why do you ask?"

"Perhaps you could finish fixing your coffee and sit down before we continue," Ralston interrupted.

I added some sugar to my cup and turned back to the table. I pulled out a chair and sat opposite the two agents. Simpson looked at me carefully, I was already convinced they knew about the bag in my truck. Simpson didn't blink before adding, "You seem a little worried Eugene, something on your mind?"

"No sir, just a little concerned. I ain't never had the FBI call in before let alone twice in a week."

"We understand" Ralston said, his tone conciliatory and friendly. "Have you seen Chase Barnwell at all in the last few days?"

"No sir, I ain't seen him in a while, kinda try not to see him if possible," I added.

"Why is that?"

"Bit a history between the Claytons and Barnwells."

"So you'd say there was some ill will between you and Chase Barnwell?" Simpson asked.

"Not on my part sir, but he never liked me. It's just some ancient feud, I never took part in, my pa never liked me not joining in."

"Ok Eugene, you absolutely sure Chase Barnwell has not been around here?" asked Ralston.

"Sure, I am," I said. "I only had old Pete Gill here to help me with some fencing, the Sheriff paid me a visit too." That made Simpson sit a little straighter.

"What did the Sheriff want?" Ralston asked.

I suddenly caught myself and took a nervous sip of my coffee. "He wanted..." I fell silent before Ralston more sternly said, "Wanted what Eugene?"

Wondering if I had stepped on the FBI equivalent of a landmine I found the words that had stuck in my throat. "He wanted to know if I had seen Chase..." My voice seemed to fall away at the end.

There were a few moments of silence before Ralston just said "Really..." his voice rising registering surprise.

Simpson interrupted sternly "We told you to let us know, if anyone came asking questions."

"Well I figured that didn't include the local Sheriff," I said regaining some strength in my voice.

Ralston glanced at Simpson before continuing, "I guess that's fair enough." With that he stood and walked over to the window that looked out to the yard. He seemed to be gathering his thoughts rather than looking at anything in particular. When he turned he looked at Simpson. If I had not been so worried about Simpson I might not have noticed the tiniest of nods of the head. That seemed to be the signal for them both to relax.

"Well Eugene you probably won't realise this but you may have inadvertently added to the family feud. Chase Barnwell gave your name as an alibi."

Of all the things he could have said that I was not expecting that statement would have been so far down the list I would have struggled to guess it if I lived to be a hundred.

"An alibi, me?" I asked, my voice incredulous.

"Yup, he did, added to which his father concurred that's what had taken place."

Pulling the chair back to sit down again Agent Ralston said, "Let me explain Eugene. You see we found the two people we came here to ask you about a couple of days ago, we tracked them down to some hut up in the forest. By the time we go there we found a couple of dead bodies and one man with a bullet wound in the leg, Chase Barnwell and another guy we have yet to identify tied to a chair clearly the subject of some aggressive interrogation. What we managed to discover from Chase Barnwell is the two were in search of a stolen bag of money. Barnwell and his gang clearly had no idea who they were dealing with, so he was in quite a state of shock when we spoke to him. Given what he saw he was all too willing to tell us about a couple of guys who joined one of their stud poker games, lost a lot of money and then seemingly disappeared."

Ralston paused briefly again glancing at Simpson seemingly for clearance to continue.

"Thing is we didn't believe everything Chase Barnwell told us. We believe Chase Barnwell spent quite a bit of time looking out for marks to invite into a poker group with his gang, one of them was an excellent cheat at cards. They'd take the mark down for whatever they had. If they failed to do it at poker they would simply do it at gun point."

It was hard to tell if my face gave away my thoughts but I was astonished to hear that Barnwell was basically a thief.

"Turns out the two we were looking for were the latest marks. From what we've learnt they were seeking out the poker game. We don't know how they found out about the game, but we have some ideas. Anyway, they turned up for the game and Barnwell and his crew got more than they bargained for. Lucky for him and the guy in the chair we arrived when we did."

Ralston paused, again glancing at Simpson before continuing. "As it turned out we got more than we bargained for as well. When we searched the building we found not only a lot of money, but a heap of cigarettes stored out back. Now the only reason anyone has that amount of tobacco is to transport it out of the State to sell somewhere like New York City. So we got us a gang of smugglers."

"And a bargaining chip with the ATF," Simpson added, a smile briefly crossing his face. Maybe he was human after all.

"The problem was we had fingerprints and other evidence all over the place for the dead guys and the one in the chair. We also had evidence to point to someone else, someone rather surprising but not for Chase Barnwell. Everything pointed to Chase being involved but he is sticking to the line that he was with you. Asking around that seemed unlikely and now you have confirmed you didn't seem him. Our chief would probably not be pleased with us sharing this so I'd appreciate you keeping things quiet, not that we anticipate you being asked anything further."

With that both men got to their feet.

"Thanks for your help Eugene," Ralston said as they headed for the door. I followed them outside and to their vehicle. As they were about to get in Ralston turned back to me.

"By the way, the mystery man was Chase Barnwell's father, so guess your town's going to be needing a new Sheriff." Ralston got in the SUV and fired up the motor.

Before joining Ralston in the vehicle Simpson called out over the roof, "There is one other thing, if you find anything unusual, like cash for example, don't bother calling us, we've enough to do what we need." With that he was in the SUV.

As the GMC headed away from my place I stood for a while slack-jawed. Things in Grayson County would never be quite the same again.

Eugene's First Vacation

As the seatbelt signs flashed on the cabin crew began their preparations for landing. Making their way down the length of the cabin collecting the last remaining glasses and remnants from the in flight service. The passenger in seat number 17C glanced slightly nervously to his right. He was in the aisle seat so his view out of the window was not great; first it was obscured by the large man in the middle seat who had been squeezing him the whole flight and second the cloud was thick in parts. The female attendant with the retro hair approached him with a professional smile pinned to her face. She reached down to the lift the plastic glass from his table and pushed the table up to fasten it. "I just need you to close the table at this time sir," she said politely. He smiled politely back, his own smile slightly forced. "Thank you m'am," he said in response before glancing back down and checking his seatbelt was tight for the umpteenth time. He tightened it fractionally.

Looking again towards the window this time he could see the occasional glimpse of the land below through occasional breaks in the cloud which seemed to increase in frequency. His stomach lurched in tune with the aircraft as it hit a small bit of turbulence caused by the warm air below. His breathing came a little more quickly as he heard an unexpected rumble and a sudden electronic whirl directly beneath him. Unaware the sound was the undercarriage coming down ready for landing he looked around at his fellow passengers all had a calm outward appearance. The cabin attendants were equally calm heading back to the front of the aircraft. He took a deep breath and tried to regain his composure. The PA system suddenly burst into life, this time the pilots voice. "Cabin crew, seats for landing please." There was another sudden lurch of the aircraft, the right wing dipping downward as if making some kind of weird salute to the earth below. The passenger in seat 17C wasn't sure if the United Airlines flight attendants were at all worried, he'd never been on a plane before. The girl who had collected his glass was certainly pretty he thought; her 1960's retro haircut would not have looked out of place in a Motown trio. The aircraft touched down with a heavy thump, the passenger suddenly worried once more, his concern raised yet further as the pilot put the aircrafts engines into reverse thrust. The twin Pratt and Witney turbines developing an enormous roar before the sound started easing in time with the sudden slowing of the aircraft. As the airplane began to swing off the runway the PA came to life once more this time with the voice of one of the cabin attendants. "Ladies and gentleman, welcome to Chicago's O'Hare International airport. Please remain seated with your seatbelt fastened at this time." Outside the aircraft the weather was reasonably bright, the early spring sun warm through the breaks in the clouds. The airport as usual was extremely busy, all six runways in use throwing planes of all sizes into the sky, some like the Boeing 737 used by United on short trips to other US cities, others much larger setting off for more far flung destinations.

Not only was this Eugene Clayton's first flight, it was the first time he had visited a large city. He had been to Louisville Kentucky whilst still at high school but Chicago was about ten times the size, he was a little apprehensive. This trip was the latest in a long line of firsts that had taken place over the last twelve months. It could be said this is no surprise given that Eugene was born and raised in a place so small it barely figured on a map, even the nearest interstate to Grayson had only one sign noting the direction from the exit ramp. With a population of 1,250 people, one decent bar and a few assorted stores, there was little point in anyone seeking to visit Grayson and as if constrained by its anonymity hardly anyone brought up there bothered to go far away, there was little use for road signs. Eugene was sure if the whole place fell into a sink hole no one outside the County would either know or care.

In a year of firsts Eugene's trip to Chicago was his first vacation. It had been old Pete's suggestion he take a trip although Pete had Florida in mind not Chicago, that was Eugene's idea, the origins of which Pete could not fathom.

The whole enterprise had begun with the first unexpected event in Eugene's life. In somewhat mysterious circumstances his dog Boris found a bag whilst rooting around in a small wood, close by where Eugene was fixing some fencing, nearby a ditch in which Eugene had come close to being shot and another man had been. The trauma of that night was eased with the discovery of the bag and more to the point its contents. A pile of cash.

At first he had been tempted to turn the bag over to the local Sheriff but on reflection he felt it might not be the best idea. Sheriff Barnwell was not a huge fan of the Clayton's, although it was Eugene's late father for whom he held most contempt. The few weeks that had preceded the discovery had been strange to say the least. Not only had he nearly been shot but he had visits from the FBI and even Sheriff Barnwell attempting to cosy up to him. All it seemed searching for a mystery couple responsible for a variety of crimes across several States. That in turn led to the discovery of another gang involved in Tobacco smuggling and more serious narcotics, all apparently with the connivance of the Sheriff who was now serving a long term in the State penitentiary. His errant son Chase Barnwell was also being hunted by the Feds but he had managed to disappear.

The weirdest thing for Eugene to grasp was not so much that he had found the money but that the Feds seemed to be both aware he had found it or might find it and happy to let him keep it. After some thought he had told old Pete, or to give him his full name Peter Gill, a long time family friend who had become something of a father figure to Eugene following his real father's death.

The two of them had counted the money and decided to stop when they reached $250,000 with a layer of bank rolls still to go. Pete suggested he put some of the funds in the bank and make a few investments into the farm, replacing a tractor and other equipment, although Eugene could not bring himself to part with his old Chevy pickup. Pete also suggested he arrange the vacation and had found someone to look after the farm whilst he had his break.

One purchase Eugene had been happy to make for himself was a computer. He had never used one before so he arranged for the young geeky kid at the store to come by and help him set it up and show him some of the basics.

The computer was the catalyst for his vacation to Chicago and not sunny Florida. After a few days familiarising himself he had registered with a number of social network sites and in turn that is how he met Lena. They had chatted online for some time before speaking via Skype, Eugene was amazed how attractive she was when they finally got from messaging and onto speaking. He was just as amazed that she seemed to find him equally appealing.

He had dated a girl once not long after leaving high school but like so many people without a family business to join she had decided to opt for the bright lights and moved to the state capital Charleston. If you can call Charleston West Virginia bright lights, but compared to Grayson anything was bright and exciting. Since then he had no meaningful girl in his life.

He was due to meet Lena for the first time tomorrow.

With the plane coming to a stop the cabin was suddenly full of activity as impatient passengers got to their feet with the big guy next to Eugene all but climbing over him to get into the aisle. For his part Eugene was slightly non plussed by the goings on and failed to grasp the urgency. Suddenly the PA burst into life again.

"Ladies and Gentlemen welcome to Chicago where the local time is 1pm Central time, one hour behind the time in Knoxville, so please remember to adjust your watches. We will soon be ready to disembark the aircraft from the forward cabin door and I would like to thank you for flying United Airlines and we hope to see you flying the friendly skies again in the near future. On behalf of Captain Timms and the rest of the crew I wish you a safe onward journey and look forward to welcoming you back to the friendly skies. Have a good day."

Now the rush began in earnest, catching on quickly Eugene unfastened his seat belt and stood to retrieve his small carryon bag from the overhead locker. He noticed when the flight was boarding that his bag was tiny compared to most passengers and he wondered whether he was travelling light or everyone else somewhat heavy.

The movement towards the front began to accelerate as the passengers made their way from the plane. Joining in line he decided to follow a guy dressed in a suit pulling a fancy looking bag and a briefcase, figuring he knew what he was doing. As they walked down the pier

111

and out into the main concourse of the arrivals terminal the first thing that struck Eugene was the vastness of the place, the second was the staggering numbers of people, most seeming to be in a hurry.

"Jeez," he said only slightly under his breath. He looked around and almost lost the guy in the suit as he scampered off ahead of him. Chasing to catch up another first confronted him, a moving walk way. As he stepped on it he almost lost his balance. Thankfully suit guy stood still and held onto the hand rail so Eugene copied him and took the chance to look around him. The building was a long yet wide space, the roof curving towards the walls making it feel more like an oversized cigar tube than a building. There were departure gates on each side, in between them various food and drink outlets and a few fancy stores selling high end clothes and the like.

Gaping around he never saw the end of the walkway, suddenly he was moving forward from the waist up but his feet didn't respond and he stumbled to the floor nearly dragging the woman and her trolley who were directly behind him down too.

"Fuck," he said, this time none too quietly attracting the attention of a group of guys standing by a bar. They burst out laughing as Eugene scrambled to his feet and walked on rapidly trying to disguise his embarrassment.

He found the baggage carousel with greater ease than he imagined he would, the suit guy had long since disappeared. As he stood waiting for the conveyor belt to produce his bag he realised why everyone on board seemed to have such large bags. He was among a very small group of people waiting in the baggage hall for luggage, clearly hardly anyone had checked on a bag.

The wait seemed interminable, the carousel had been turning for several minutes before the first bag arrived and for what seemed a lifetime the first bag was the sole bag on the belt. It passed Eugene twice before others began to join it almost as if by magic, arriving through the rubber curtain in the wall.

Whilst waiting he pulled the small map and his written instructions of how to get to downtown Chicago and locate his hotel from his jacket pocket . His first task was to get himself on the train into the city. Looking behind he saw the signs above the exit door with arrowed directions to parking areas, hotel shuttle buses, taxis and on the right hand side the Chicago Transit Authority sign for the "L" service. The momentary distraction ensured the safe arrival of his small case, it like so much of the contents a very recent purchase.

Finding the train was a synch, buying a ticket however was not. The ticket machine was way too complicated and it must have been designed and built by a midget, Eugene who at five ten was no giant had to get to his knees to read the instructions. He might as well have not bothered because he could not follow them. He was not alone, each machine had a confused tourist in front of it.

Fortunately CTA staff were on hand to help and a tall member of staff made his way over, Eugene wondered how he was going to bend low enough to see the machine, the guy looked like he belonged on a basketball court.

"Where you goin' sir?" he asked.

Eugene glanced briefly at the paper in his hand just to be sure. "I need to get to Washington and Lake."

The tall guy bent double and pressed a couple of buttons on the machine before rising to his full height. Looking down at Eugene he pointed to the right side of the machine. "You can pay through there with cash, or," lifting his finger fractionally to another slot in the machine, "there with a credit card, either way sir it'll be two dollars and fifty cents. Have a great day."

Fitting his cash into the slot Eugene gathered his ticket and made his way through the entrance gates, scanning his ticket via the reader the same way he saw those in front of him do. He got down to the platform where he needed to take the blue line into the city. He should not have worried it seems only the blue line comes out to the airport.

The CTA described their service to the city as a rapid transit and Eugene was struggling to understand what was rapid about it as the service made its way slowly between the first stops of Rosemont and Cumberland.

By the time the train had reached the Washington and Lake station Eugene was extremely bored with the trip. The only thing he found surprising on the ride was the run down appearance of some of the properties that backed on to the line. Many looked like the kind of run down places found in the backwoods of home, not what he expected in what he assumed must be a prosperous city.

Getting off the train and leaving the station was easier than getting on and he quickly found himself in what he could only assume was some sort of shopping mall. He followed exit signs to the top of a down escalator which surprised him as he had just got off a train that had travelled below street level so to go down again was not what he expected. With no choice but to take it he rode down to an area full of stores and helpfully a large map with a 'You are here' note that helped him to navigate his way to the street.

Once outside he was suddenly awestruck. The afternoon was bright with sun yet a street level it was almost dark, the buildings blocking the sunlight. Eugene had seen plenty of tall buildings on TV shows but nothing prepared him for this. For a moment he felt not just awed by the sight but almost intimidated by the scale of the place.

Looking up and down the street he realised he had not paid attention to the map and the directions for his hotel which was on West Madison St. With no clue which way was which he walked to his right in what he figured was roughly west. At the end of the block he looked for the name of the street but could not see a sign. He crossed the street and carried on the next block hoping to find himself but could only locate St. Peters Church, the place looked incongruous wedged between the monster high rises, a throw back to an earlier time. Walking on to the end of the block he discovered he was at West Calhoun Place and totally lost.

With little alternative he walked and crossed to the next block. Up ahead he could see a sign for another station for the "L" and out front a taxi stand.

He walked up to the first taxi, the driver was lost on his smart phone, engrossed in something or other. Eugene did not have a smart phone, in fact he had only got a cell phone because Pete Gill reckoned he should.

They had picked it up a store on the interstate as they ran down to Knoxville. It was in his bag and he had not even turned it on. As he tapped on the passenger side window the driver looked up with the broadest smile Eugene had ever seen. He opened the rear door, tossed his bag in and followed it onto to the seat.

"Where to?" asked the driver.

Since he could not pronounce the name of the hotel properly Eugene handed the driver his printed itinerary. The guy took it and his eyes rolled to the top of his head, his broad smile turned to a roar of laughter.

"Is there something wrong?" Eugene asked.

"No, sir, but you in for the shortest cab ride you ever had. I take it you new in town," he said, turning the ignition key and firing up the engine. "Your hotel is about a block and half behind us and is probably quicker to walk than the ride since we gotta take the one way streets."

Feeling slightly embarrassed Eugene also laughed, although his sounded a little nervous. He looked at the driver's mirror and saw the guy was still grinning from one ear to the next. He was the blackest guy Eugene had ever seen and his accent was like none he had ever heard. "You got me, definitely new in town and I ain't never been in no city before. You from round here?"

"Yes sir, live about halfway out of the city on the south side, but I'm from Ghana."

"Ghana? Ain't heard a' that, which state is Ghana?"

This time Eugene though the guy's laugh would blow the doors off the cab. "Well mister, you really done no travelling. Ghana is in West Africa, I been in your beautiful country for five years now."

Eugene's embarrassment was replaced by a sense of shame at his own ignorance. He sat for a few moments silently trying to work out what to say. The cab had pulled up at a set of stop lights before making a right, followed by another. As they turned Eugene looked up and saw the street name, West Madison St. Laughing he said, "Well, you were right about the ride being short."

"Yes sir, your hotel is on the next block."

"Thank you, and I'm sorry I had never heard of Ghana before, guess my life has been pretty much wrapped up in the goin's on of my small town in West Virginia." As he finished speaking the cab rolled to a stop outside his hotel. He looked at the meter and saw the sign read $3.50, he peeled a five dollar note from his roll and handed to the driver. As the guy reached for his money belt Eugene added, "No sir, you keep that."

"Thank you sir, have a nice day."

Closing the door and turning towards the hotel in one movement Eugene stole a brief glance back at the taxi. The driver was still beaming, he figured it must be a permanent smile. So much to learn he thought as he pushed the hotel door open.

Once in his room Eugene threw his bag on the bed and walked to the window, he was on the twenty first floor and could see little below him, with not much to see above either he turned away and decided he would go for a walk. But only after he had found a map.

He made his way to the hotel lobby which was actually on the seventeenth floor. He had never been in a hotel before but he always assumed the front entrance and lobby would be at ground floor level not halfway to the sky.

The girl on the front desk was very helpful and went through a few places he might visit and drew some circles around the places she mentioned, providing him with clear directions to find the Millennium Park and, given it required him to step out on to the street, turn left and walk in a straight line. He figured this was the safest option.

The walk was only a handful of blocks and in no time he was in the park and headed across it towards the lake shore. He had decided, despite the girl's recommendations, to ignore the museums and instead walked along the water's edge. Although there was a stiff wind blowing the temperature was good and he did not feel at all cold.

Old Pete had told him the wind always blew in Chicago and especially off the lake. He also told him that the city was not known as 'the Windy City' because of the wind that but had acquired its nickname in the nineteenth century, although some debate as to who actually named it first the term was used in reference to the city's politicians and the amount of hot air they expressed. Eugene often wondered if there was anything old Pete did not know.

As he walked his thoughts turned to Lena, he was really looking forward to meeting her for the first time even though he was a tad nervous. Gazing out to the lake he wondered what she was doing now. He knew she would be at work, she worked in an office in a place called Waukegan, about an hours drive north of Chicago. She told him she was able to walk to work from her apartment. Apart from that, her pretty face and that she was originally from somewhere in Russia having moved to the States with her family when she was very young, Eugene knew little about her.

Despite having not eaten much since he had left home that morning he did not feel in the least bit hungry, besides he had not seen a single place serving fried chicken. So far all he had seen on the food front was a couple of weird sounding places with even weirder sounding food. He figured he could manage until he found some chicken or ribs.

He found a small bench seat by the water's edge and sat for a while watching sail boats and fancy looking machines with engines racing back and forth. He wondered if he could have a ride in a boat, it looked like he might enjoy it. He made a mental note to ask Lena if she fancied a trip.

The paved walkway was busy with other folk doing pretty much the same as him, with more athletic types out jogging. Eugene had never fancied jogging for the sake of it since he had never seen a jogger smile he figured it was not in the least bit enjoyable. Every now and again someone would shoot by on rollerblades or a strange looking two wheel contraption he had never seen before. The rider was standing up holding on to a pair of bars, the machine could sure shift. Later he saw one standing on its own and noted it was called a Segway. It just looked dangerous to Eugene; he decided this was one experience he could live without.

Whilst he had been watching the wind had strengthened and he noticed the effect this had on the lake. Waves were forming in growing clusters, their tops turning white. He looked at the sailboats more carefully and saw how they leaned away from the wind; he thought they might topple over. The racy ones with engines had suddenly reduced in number, those that were still around rose and fell on the waves like a rodeo ride. Maybe it ain't such a fun thing?, he said slightly aloud.

The wind seemed to be getting stronger by the minute and although the sky was clear of clouds he was suddenly feeling cold. He zipped up his thin jacket before standing to start to walk back into the city. As he headed back across Millennium Park the wind provided a boost to his speed, almost as though mother nature was telling him it was a good idea to get away. Glancing over his shoulder he noticed how the numbers of people around the place had thinned considerably.

By the time Eugene got back to his hotel he was feeling much warmer, not because the wind had eased, but due to the pace of his return walk. He figured the wind was worse in the canyon like streets as it whipped itself into a frenzy accelerating between the buildings, it's velocity almost malevolent. The traffic had also built up as the end of the working day brought people out from their cosy warm offices to begin the commute home. Streams of people heading for the "L", nursing take out coffee's, their coats fastened against the cold.

For the first time Eugene felt genuinely hungry but had little desire to venture far. He'd noticed a little place across the street calling itself an Italian Steakhouse, whatever the heck one of those was but he figured he would find something edible for dinner.

He pushed open the door and was immediately confused as the place looked more like a sports bar, clearly looking out of place a woman in the black uniform of the wait staff came over and asked if he was looking for a table. She showed him to a table by the window and handed him a menu, returning a short while later and filled his glass with iced water.

"Can I get you anything to drink? And have you made a choice for food?"

Although not averse to alcohol Eugene rarely drank but said to her, "As I'm on vacation, I'll take a beer please." In reply she rattled out a list of beers he had never heard of so he settled for a Budweiser. The food on the menu looked equally confusing, loads of fancy names and things sounding nothing like food he had ever come across. Looking down the list he did see some Chicken Wings but they came with a strange sounding sauce which he reckoned was probably nothing like the sauce he got at Harry's Place back home in Grayson. With no ribs or pork of any kind he recognised on the menu he ordered the only other thing he knew, "And a burger and fries please."

He struggled to remember the last time he had eaten a burger that had not come out of his freezer when he had one of those evenings that he stayed home and indulged his only cooking ability, using a microwave.

Since he was due to stay in Chicago for five days he was deeply concerned he would not find any decent food.

The following day Eugene was awake early as usual, the first glimmer of dawn barely visible outside his hotel window. He was due to meet Lena at ten o'clock at a Starbucks just by her stop on the "L", she had told him she would drive to a place called Howard and take the train from there as she did not want to drive in the city.

After taking a long shower and spending more time in the bathroom than he could remember spending before he was still ready to go to breakfast by seven. The hotel served breakfast in a small section of the lobby. Fortunately for Eugene he recognised pretty much everything on offer. Taking a plate of eggs and bacon from the buffet he felt better about his dietary needs than he had the day before. The eggs and bacon were so good he went back for a second helping. By the time he left the table he was fully nourished and close to being awash with coffee.

He took the elevator to street level and stepped outside, the wind had abated and once again the spring weather was warm and he felt a surge of excitement for the day that lay ahead. He had decided to take a walk to try and pass the time before he was due to meet Lena but it seemed to drag, he looked at his watch incessantly and willed time to pass more quickly. With little interest in what he was doing he was at the Starbucks just before nine, a line of office workers who were piling out with giant mugs of coffee in hand as they scampered to their desks. Walking through the door Eugene quickly realised the line started just inside leading to the counter, the serving area, the sugar stand and then back out the door. It snaked its way around the inside of the building between seating areas and people apparently set up to work with lap top computers and all sorts of other paraphernalia laid out. Joining in the shuffle he looked up at the board above the servers and was again bamboozled by what he saw. Among a list of complicated names that he thought referred to men's pants his eyes fell on something he recognised as a coffee and decided he would order one of those.

With his Americano in hand Eugene stepped over to a raised counter and pulled up a stool to sit and wait for Lena.

Lena Zinchenko was at that moment buying a ticket to ride the purple line of the "L" into downtown Chicago for her long arranged meeting with Eugene Clayton. She was almost besides herself with excitement, she had spent a long time in online chatrooms, social web sites and dating sites she had yet to find anything meaningful. This time however she was confident all was about to change and her life alter forever.

Stepping onto the train she attracted a lot of looks, she usually did. At five feet eight inches, with her slim figure, her already long legs seemed endless when adorned with the four inch heels she had on. Her dark hair was long, thick and shone like a polished gemstone. Although Eugene thought she was Russian she was actually from Odessa in the Ukraine. She had decided it was too complicated to try and explain about the Ukraine. Although not the first country that sprang to mind when considering where the most beautiful women in the world originate the Ukraine was right up there with places like Sweden in magazine surveys. Lena knew how good she looked and made sure she took full advantage.

Taking her seat and pretending not to notice the admiring glances she ceremoniously crossed her right leg over her left, took her iPhone out of her pocket and checked on her emails and messages. She had one, her reply was short and to the point, "On the way."

Looking around the café Eugene could tell some people seemed to make a coffee last an awfully long time. His was long since finished but he decided not to order another as he was high enough already, any more coffee and he might just embarrass himself when Lena arrived. He looked at his watch again, 9.55, just five minutes to go; she could arrive any moment.

From his seat he could see across the street to the exit from the station so it was no surprise that he saw her come out onto the street. At least he was sure it was her, he had seen her on Skype several times and there was no way he could forget that face.

What surprised him was how tall, slim and elegant she looked. Men turned to look at her, one stumbling and nearly falling into the oncoming traffic, the blare of the vehicle horns loud enough to wake the dead. She walked to the street corner and waited for the crossing light to go green. He watched her head over the street, his heart beginning to race, his excitement almost uncontrollable. Easing himself from his stool he tried to look as calm and cool as possible. He was like a swan, on the surface moving easily, under the water his legs working overtime to keep him going. He thought his heart might burst at any moment.

When Lena walked through the front door the whole place stopped, both sexes stared at her. With a gulp Eugene walked to meet her, both their faces breaking into smiles of recognition.

As they drew close Lena placed a hand on Eugene's right arm and leant into him brushing her lips against his right cheek. His face flushed bright red, he was sure the entire place was staring at him. In truth they were not, most of the occupants had turned back to whatever they were doing, it was only a few men who continued to look at Lena a sense of wonder coursing through their minds as they reflected on what *she was doing with him?*

"Hi, how are you?" Eugene managed to stammer. "So good to see you, meet you even."

"Likewise," she said, her accent no longer contained any trace of her Ukrainian roots. "I am just great thank you and all the better for finally meeting you."

If it was remotely possible to Eugene managed to turn even redder. His heart pounding now, he could feel the blood in his head bouncing against the skull as though it wanted to get out. He had never been so excited in his life.

He took a deep breath in an effort to control his voice. He knew he was meant to take the lead now, be the gentlemen, he'd seen things on TV and he had a faint memory of his mother talking to a friend about how she wished her husband treated her with more respect and behaved like a gentleman, rather than the asshole he was. Eugene had been young at the time and guessed he wasn't supposed to hear his mother on the telephone that day. But she was sure right he thought, my father was a complete asshole. Banishing that thought he concentrated on the moment in hand.

"What would you like to do?" he asked. He had gone over and over various things they might do together that day but had singularly failed to make a concrete plan. After all he really didn't know Lena well enough to decide what she might like to do most.

"Why don't we have a coffee while we think about it?" she said, taking his arm and steering him towards the back of the coffee line. Pointing to the board she told him the complicated sounding drink she wanted. Eugene glanced at her and asked, "Is that really coffee, or somethin' else?"

She laughed gently and squeezed his arm as she leant closer to him and kissed him gently on the cheek. "Yes, its coffee." She giggled again and turned to go in search of a table.

The smell of her perfume and the feeling of her lips against his cheek sent his heart racing flat out again, like he had just chased NFL running back Chris Johnson down a 40 yard stretch. Eugene watched him play a few times when he was at the Tennessee Titans, boy was he quick.

Collecting his coffee and her chino thingy Eugene walked over to the table she had secured in the window. The view out the window on this side was a little odd as the street was nearly dark with the Loop part of the "L" system riding on its steel stilts down the centre of the street, ensuring what little light past the skyscrapers was reduced yet more.

Once seated they both just looked at each other, gazing in silence, neither quite able to believe their luck.

"So Eugene Clayton, what would you like to do?" She asked.

Now he was stuck, he had to think of something. He spoke a little hesitantly. "Well, I'm not sure, I looked at all kinds of things and just couldn't make a decision. Ain't been in this situation before."

"How about I make a suggestion?"

"Sure that'd be good."

"Why don't we finish our coffees and take a walk down to the park. We can catch the train there and ride up the lakeshore a little and I know there are some nice places to eat up near there where we can look out to the lake."

"Will they serve chicken or ribs? I ain't seen anything I usually eat on any menus."

Lena laughed gently, "I'm sure there will be, but I intend to help you broaden your southern diet a little."

Finishing up their coffees they left through the side door and turned left to head towards Millennium Park. After they had taken a few steps Lena reached down and took hold of Eugene's hands. His whole body tingled at the sensation.

Although it is not that far to the park they took an age as they walked, stopping and looking into shop fronts and talking about all kinds of things, Eugene already knew Lena liked tennis and most sport in general. For his part he was a complete sports nut, although baseball was probably his favourite having played a lot at school. His throwing arm still powerful, mostly down to work on the farm and fighting off his occasionally violent father in days gone by.

Every now and then they just stopped and talked, gazing at each other like loves young dream. Eugene could not believe his luck when he first came across Lena online, now as his heart threatened to explode he was simply lost in a world he thought of as make believe.

By the time they reached the South Shore Line station at the park he was actually feeling faint. He wondered if he was falling in love though he had no idea what that was. Lena could have taken him anywhere and he would simply follow like a lost puppy.

Lena bought tickets for the train whilst Eugene stood back admiring her and glowing in the attention she attracted. If he could he would shout out loud, "She's mine", but he decided he better not. She led lead the way onto the train and they found two empty seats together. She told him the ride was not long and they would have plenty of time to scout the restaurants and bars to find somewhere he fancied to eat.

It seemed to Eugene they had hardly been on the train a few minutes when the tannoy announced the next station was Belmont. They stepped off the train and made their way through the narrow station building into a parking lot. Assuming they would head on foot towards the exit Eugene was a little surprised that Lena headed towards the parking lot and a Japanese compact that looked like it had seen better days.

"Are we not walking?"

"No honey, it's a little further than we walked in downtown so I thought a ride would be easier."

The term compact seemed to have been invented for this auto Eugene thought as he adjusted the seat to give his legs a little more room. Although no midget he hardly thought himself tall and yet he could only just get in. He looked at the driver's seat and the instruments and spotted the name Nissan, not a make he had ever been in before.

They set off to the lot exit and made a left which seemed to be away from the direction Eugene assumed they would head. Saying nothing to begin with it was only after they had travelled a mile or so that he broke his silence. "We seem to be going west, I figured the beach was probably north."

"Sorry honey, I should have said I just need to go to my apartment on the way I forgot something."

They drove on a few more miles travelling beneath what he assumed was an interstate highway before making a number of turns, Eugene was slightly confused about where they were now. The only thing he was sure of with the sun directly in front of them is they were headed in a southerly direction, the houses in the area tightly packed together. Eugene imagined it would be possible to reach out of a window in any of the houses and reach its neighbour. A moment later Lena turned right and they headed along the back of a row of houses, each with a wooden fronted garage before coming to a halt on the right side outside the last on a small block.

"Here we are, would you like to come in and see where I live?"

She opened her door and swung her long elegant legs out of the door. Eugene followed suit and waited for her to step around the back of the car. Lena led the way up a narrow path that they accessed through a very worn looking wooden gate held upright by being closed.

As soon as they were through she had to lift the gate slightly to close it. The building was part brick and part wood, it stood next to two similar three storey properties. The rest of the street seemed to be small houses with slightly larger yards and garages.

The rear stairs that doubled as a fire exit were easier to use than walking round front as that involved walking the length of the block Lena explained. Her apartment was the on the first floor.

The apartment was narrow and long and only had one bedroom. They entered the property through the kitchen which was across the whole of the back of the property. There was one door in the center of the opposite wall, she led him through the door into a narrow corridor. To the left was what he figured was the bathroom and bedroom as there were two doors on the left of the corridor. She took the single door on the right, as they walked through Eugene saw the desktop computer opposite him and looked behind him to the way he had stepped in and immediately recognised a mirror on the wall he had seen during their Skype calls.

"What do you think?" Lena asked.

"I knew where I was as soon as we came in the room," he said indicating the mirror on the wall.

"Great, could you just wait here a minute I just need to go to the bathroom?" Without waiting for a reply she walked out of the room closing the door behind her.

Eugene walked over to the small front window and was looking out on the street, his back to the door when he heard it open. Turning to speak to Lena he was stunned to see a giant of a man walk through the door.

The words he was about to utter died on his lips as Eugene took in the sight before him. For the second time in a year he was looking at the wrong end of a gun. His bowels made an involuntary movement and his face became clammy. His mind went back to that night in the ditch. Visions of blood and guts flashed into his mind, the screams of the guy he witnessed being killed filled his head. His eyes were fixed on the gun

"Hello Eugene, we meet at last," the giant said.

Eugene was at once perplexed as well as terrified as his gaze continued to rest on the terrifying looking weapon. What did this guy mean we meet at last?

"I so enjoyed the way you came onto me in our online chats, all that southern charm. If I was gay I might even give you a try."

Eugene's mind was whirring. Who the hell was this guy? What is he talking about? Distracted by the giant's comments Eugene's concern at the gun started to turn to despair as he started to realise he might have been duped.

"I can see you look a little baffled Eugene, you didn't think Lena was really interested in a country boy like you did you? This was only ever a business arrangement for her." Suddenly raising his voice he added, "Isn't that right darling?"

Darling? What was going on Eugene thought. His thoughts were suddenly interrupted as the door opened once more as in stepped Lena looking very different, her hair now pulled back most of her make up removed. She looked almost plain. Gone to were the heels, replaced by flat shoes and the skirt had been exchanged for a pair of jeans. "I am sorry Eugene, I am not what you think. This is nothing personal, as Andrei said, this is just business."

Her voice sounded different to Eugene, an edge had crept in, almost cold. Continuing she said, "So we need to get on with why we are here. Eugene I need you to step over to the computer for me please."

"Why would I do that?"

"Well it is really very simple, we need you to go into your bank account and transfer all that lovely money you so fortunately found and give it to us. If you don't I cannot be sure what Andrei here will do."

Eugene actually laughed. Even to him in those circumstances it seemed stupid, but laughing was all he could think of.

"I don't think you realise how much trouble you are in Eugene, this is no joke." Lena said before Andrei interrupted her. "Move to the computer and get into your bank account otherwise I will shoot you."

"Shoot me, with that?" He replied pointing at the enormous gun almost rendered toy like in the huge fist of Andrei. "Shoot me with that thing in here and the bullet will probably pass straight through me, then the wall and hit who knows who outside. That would be pretty dumb. So you ain't gonna shoot me. I don't think you are that dumb."

At that moment Eugene wondered if in fact it was him who was being dumb as Andrei stepped quickly across to him and struck him a mighty blow to the side of the head with the gun. The blow knocked him to the floor, as he fell he narrowly avoided striking his head on a low level cupboard. He put his arms out to break the fall, they only succeeded in slowing his fall to the floor.

He lay still for some time. His head spun, his hearing seemed effected, he heard a muffled voice. The only clear sound was his own groan but that could have been in his head. His eyes misted slightly, the light momentarily fading. The blow was hard, just hard enough to be painful and not sufficient to render him unconscious. He could feel something moist behind his ear however the cut was not too deep. As he started to lift himself on to his elbows he felt a strong arm under his suddenly pull him up.

Once on his feet he could see the huge revolver was now in the hands of Lena, firmly held in a two handed grip. The giant hauled him across to the computer and put Eugene in the chair in front of the screen. He pushed the power button on the PC and then stepped away taking the gun back from Lena before stepping back to Eugene's side.

"Now funny guy, you get into your account and arrange to transfer all the money to the account noted on the pad beside the keyboard. Do you understand?"

Eugene's speech was slightly slurred. "Oh, I understand okay. Unfortunately, it's you that don't. I ain't got an online bank account."

"Don't fuck with me Eugene," Andrei said. "Get onto your bank and do it now."

"I can't, I really ain't got an online account," Eugene insisted. All this achieved was to earn him another blow to the head. This time with Andrei's left fist, although not as savage as the first blow it rocked Eugene who slumped forwards and slipped to the floor. Once again he felt himself hauled back up and into the chair.

"Look you can hit me as much as you like but I really ain't got an online account. I got a bank account but there's hardly any money in it. Keep most o' the money in the bag I found it in."

The room fell silent, Eugene was still staring at the computer screen unsure what was going to happen next, too worried to look round. The silence seemed to last forever but in reality it was less than a minute. Andrei broke the quiet. "Lena, fetch my tools," he commanded.

Continuing to stare at the screen Eugene concentrated hard on the sounds. He was terrified at the idea of tools being fetched. He was striving to stay alert. His eyesight had recovered and the blood trickling down his head was slowing but he now had a pounding headache made worse the harder he concentrated.

Hearing the door reopen he jumped slightly. He heard a sound as something of reasonable weight was put on the floor. "Here, hold this," he heard Andrei command and assumed he had handed Lena the gun. For the first time he wondered if Lena was her real name. The sounds that followed were faint, a tiny metallic scratching sound that caused the hairs on the back of his neck to stand up, his neck and shoulder muscles tensing in anticipation of some new horror. His hearing was now tuned in he could even discern Lena's slightly uneven breathing, the tension clearly getting to her too.

Andrei stepped over to him with a pair of plastic cuffs in his hand. Out of his peripheral vision he saw the giant of a man appear to his right. "Put your hands behind your back," he ordered. For a brief moment Eugene considered defying the instruction but his headache reminded him that disobedience now was probably not the best course of action. He slowly moved his hands behind his back, shuffling forwards slightly in the chair. As soon as his arms were behind him he felt

Andrei's big hands grab first his right wrist and then something plastic being placed over his hand and then his left wrist was grabbed and he felt the same sensation. He felt a sharp pull and his wrists were pulled tight together.

"Stay precisely where you are, we will only be the other side of the door," Andrei said. He heard them both leave the room.

Once outside Andrei said, "That was not supposed to happen."

"I know, but I think he is telling the truth. These simple country folk... What a mess, I should have thought about this more."

"Well there's no point worrying about it now, I guess you're right so we have no choice now." Andrei left the last word hanging.

"What do you mean no choice, what the heck are you thinking of doing, you're not going to kill him are you?"

"No, I mean we have no choice but to take him home and get the money."

"Drive to Virginia, are you mad? It'll take days..."

"Sure, but how long have we been planning and working on this? Months, so a few more days won't hurt. We need to move him from here, we can take him to the other place and then leave tomorrow in the van, we'll there by nightfall."

Lena looked at him apprehensively but she could see the determined look on his face and realised there was no point arguing. For her part she felt they had simply screwed up so they should do what they always intended, leave him locked up in the apartment and take off. The place was not in her real name, the rent was paid for another month. Even if Eugene went to the police by the time they had made any sense of what was going on they would both be back in Seattle in their normal lives. Losing out on the money after so much planning would be bad news, but not the end of the world. She had other marks lined up. The revised plan worried her, it worried her a lot.

Once back in the room Andrei grabbed hold of Eugene's shirt collar and pulled telling him to stand. "We are going down stairs in a moment and we are getting into the rear seats of Lena's car, one false move or noise from you and I will not hesitate to shoot you, am I clear?"

"Yes," Eugene replied. He had no idea if the guy would shoot him or not but right now he was not about to try anything to find out.

He had begun to wonder if he could possibly escape but for now simply resigned himself to going along with what he was told. The good news was they seemed to believe him about the money. Despite standing he was still facing the computer, he heard footsteps moving away and assumed Lena was leaving unless a third person had joined them. Then he heard the outside door at the back open and Andrei tugged him round. With his left arm holding Eugene's elbow and the gun in his right hand Andrei gave him a gentle push. "Walk ahead of me and go back the way you came in."

They walked out, Eugene leading as ordered. Once at the bottom of the stairs he realised there was little likelihood anyone looking at the back of the property from one of the other buildings would see much as the short path was narrow and the wooden fencing, although old and worn, was quite high. Identifying anything other than two people moving along it would be impossible.

The gate hung open at the rear and the Nissan was pulled up in line with the gate, it's rear door open. Lena was standing to the back of the car, her expression grim. As they reached the car Andrei put his left hand on Eugene's head pushing down like a police officer loading a suspect.

Continuing to be compliant Eugene got in the car and moved across to the far side, the big guy getting in after him. Lena closed the door behind him and got in the driver's side and started the car and took off.

They drove almost two hours due West. The distance between towns becoming greater and the towns smaller the further they drove. They spent a little bit of time driving on the Ronald Reagan Memorial Highway before taking an off ramp and heading South. Eugene had not spotted the sign so had no idea where they were headed, not that it would make much difference to know he thought.

They went deeper into arable farming country, the landscape flatter than a pool table with the early signs of crops appearing from the ground. Mile after mile of flat land, Eugene had never seen anything like it. The landscape was completely alien after the hills of Southern West Virginia.

More than once Eugene thought they were close to their destination as Lena slowed the auto as though she was going to turn someplace. Each time she did he figured she was double checking where she was, this was not an entirely familiar route. By the time they had been travelling for three hours the car turned off the paved road and headed down a dusty track. A few minutes later Lena turned off the track into a small farmyard which was almost entirely surrounded by trees and thick bushes, pulling up outside the house, Eugene thought it looked abandoned. The small barn across from the house was in the same forlorn state as the house. Attached to the barn was a lean to with a white GMC van parked beneath it.

Lena got out of the car and went to the barn, she unlocked a padlock and pulled the door open. Returning to the car she got in and drove directly into the barn. Inside the barn looked much tidier and more organised than Eugene had imagined. The only small hint that the place had once been an active farm was a twenty year old Massey Ferguson tractor with a front loader attached. The tractor was on the left as they drove in; an old work bench was on the right hand side long since cleared of any equipment, there was the odd rusty old tool hanging from the walls. Parked next to the tractor was a recent model Ford pickup looking pristine compared to Eugene's own beaten up Chevy.

This time when Lena stopped the car she turned the engine off got out and stepped back to the car's rear passenger door on the side Eugene was sitting and opened it before standing back.

The jab in the ribs from the gun in Andrei's hand was all the direction he needed to exit the vehicle.

Swivelling his body to allow his legs to exit before he then pushed himself up. Andrei got out the back and moved around the car before taking Eugene by the arm and leading him towards the tractor. As he did Lena produced another set of plastic cuffs. Once at the tractor Andrei pushed Eugene to sit with his back against the side of the front loader bucket. Keeping the gun pointed directly at his head whilst Lena bent down and cuffed Eugene's legs. They clearly assumed he was capable of some superhuman effort and made doubly sure he could not get away by attaching a rope to his cuffed wrists before tying the rope to the front loader arm. Without a further word they left him and walked out shutting the barn door as they did. Eugene heard the padlock being applied.

With nothing else to do Eugene tried as much as he could to relax. It was difficult to do with his wrists tightly bound, the plastic biting into the flesh, the blood flow having long since been cut off. His shoulders were now beginning to suffer with his arms pulled behind him. He could not properly lean back against the bucket to take some of the weight from his lower back. Looking up he spotted the cause of the limited light in the place as the roof had openings where skylights had once be placed, now the holes they left provided enough light for Eugene to look around, not that there was much to see from the floor. He looked left but could not see what was behind the tractor and the pickup. Every part of him was now hurting. Perhaps fortunately fatigue got the better of him and he fell asleep his head lolling to the side.

He woke with a start at the sound of the door being opened. His eyes not properly focussed he thought he saw both Andrei and Lena come into the barn. He screwed his eyes tight and blinked a couple of times before refocussing on the pair. Andrei still held the gun in his hand, but Lena was carrying a bottle of water and a plate of food. Eugene could not make out what it was but simply the sight of it made him feel hungry, his stomach growling like a bad tempered dog, letting him know how long it had been since he'd last eaten.

Lena set the plate and bottle down, before releasing the rope tying his wrists to the tractor. She produced a pair of cutters, they looked to Eugene like a small pair of wire cutters he used on the farm. She cut the ties from his wrists and his arms fell blissfully free. There was no feeling in his hands he moved his arms in front of him, his hands were almost blue. As he did Lena placed the bottle beside him and the plate next to it. The plate had some meat and potatoes on it with a fork to eat it with. Not something Eugene would normally choose to eat, but in his current condition it looked like the best plate of food he had ever seen.

Both Andrei and Lena stood back as he reached to lift the plate. He almost dropped it all as his hands felt like a useless jelly. As the blood flow returned so his hands began to hurt. To begin with he could hardly grip the fork but soon got the measure of things and ate the food greedily, before opening the water and taking a large glug to wash his food down.

Throughout his two captors watched in silence.

As soon as he had finished they both stepped over. Once again his writs were bound, this time by Lena who mercifully did not manage to pull the ties as tight as they had been previously. They also refrained from tying him to the tractor. They left and locked the barn once again.

For a while Eugene simply tried to get comfortable against the tractor bucket allowing his meal to digest. They had left the water bottle but how they expected him to drink was beyond him. He had already decided that simply waiting for whatever happened next was not an option. Without being tied to the tractor he could at least lie down and roll.

Without knowing what was hanging above the bench on the opposite wall he decided to make an effort to find out. Lying flat he rolled himself over; on the first roll he trapped his hand and the pressure on his already aching shoulder made him wince. After a couple of turns he found a useful rhythm and could keep his direction by bring his knees up towards his chest and then almost like an earth worm he could wriggle in into the correct direction. He had no idea how long it took to reach the bench but the light was fading fast.

The little Nissan was parked up close enough to the bench that he was able to place his back against the door and by pushing his feet on the cross member at the bottom of the bench and lever himself upright. The first time he did it he lost his balance and toppled over giving his already sore head another good crack to be going on with. Out of breath and in some pain he lay still for a while before gathering himself and getting upright again. This time he leant against the car for balance.

With the light almost gone he struggled to see what was above the bench. There were a number of old rusty hand tools, one an old tree lopper with a serrated blade. It was probably blunt with age but Eugene thought it had to be worth trying to see if he could free himself with it. Staring at the tool he foresaw two problems; first getting on the bench to retrieve it and second how to position it so he could rub his wrists against it. At that point the idea that he might also cut his own wrists and bleed to death had not crossed his mind.

The first challenge he realised could be overcome with the simply expedient of bouncing himself in the air

149

to sit on the bench. Hopping the short distance to the bench he turned himself and found he could almost sit on the bench with little effort as it was less than the height of his hips. Getting his backside on the bench proved straight forward and once more drawing his knees towards his chest he shuffled himself back and quickly found his back resting against the wall. He shuffled along the bench and despite gathering a number of wood splinters in his hand and butt he made it to the tree saw hanging from a small peg. So far so good he thought, but how the heck do I use it? He glanced around anxiously seeking an answer to the question.

He couldn't see one.

Andrei and Lena were in the house sitting silently, directly avoiding eye contact, almost not noticing each other. They'd had a heated argument, Lena telling him just how uncomfortable she was. Everything had gone wrong she said. It was supposed to be like the others, a simple case of having their target move the money into one of the myriad of bank accounts they had in the Cayman Islands. They had accumulated a lot of money. Eugene Clayton's new found wealth was to be the last one and then they would stop.

Their immediate plan had been to leave for Europe whilst the dust settled on the trail of victims across several states. Beyond that they had not made further plans but they knew if they just kept going eventually the police somewhere would find a lead to them. Now they had broken every rule, the worst being the cash, if they did get it what were they to do with so much cash? The rules for banks now meant they could not simply take the money into a bank to pay it in. Leaving the country with a bag of money was not likely to be as easy as it sounded.

It was Andrei who broke the silence. "We have come this far we just need to get his money then we're done."

"What are we supposed to do with so much cash?"

"We can hide some, take some with us maybe, we'll think of something."

"I'm really not sure, maybe we should just quit now, leave him here and take off?"

"Lena, I'm going to get that money, you are either with me or not." There was a finality to his voice. Pushing back his chair, Andrei left the room without another word.

Having got himself situated close enough to the tool Eugene began to think hard about how he could use it. On the plus side he thought his wrists were loose enough that he could move his hands a little and his fingers completely. On the downside he was sure he could not hold the saw and use it against the ties at the same time.

He continued looking around the barn, the back was almost completely dark now, but his eyes had adjusted well. Now he was able to see past the Nissan he could see the bench ran almost the entire length of the place. There was another, shorter bench along the back wall, it seemed misshaped, a hump in the middle of it. Maybe something under a cover he thought.

His first action was to push himself back towards the tool hanging behind him. His fingers closed around the serrated blade, he was surprised how sharp it felt. He lifted himself and his arms slightly trying to release the tool from the hook. Nothing happened.

Wriggling himself closer, he tried again. Nothing happened. A third time, again nothing. He figured he had time on his side so he was only frustrated and not the least bit anxious. He sat still for a few minutes and thought.

For his fourth attempt Eugene lifted his bound legs onto the bench and managed to get himself on his knees. With a bit more height to use he felt he could maybe lift the saw more easily. He felt behind and for a moment panic shot through him as he could not feel the saw. In the process of lifting his legs and gathering them under himself he'd moved to one side of the saw. He replayed in his mind pulling his legs up, rolling onto his right side and then tucking his legs under his butt as he wedged his head against the rear wall to act as a lever. He figured another bang on the head and more pressure was not going to make him feel any worse than he already did. Going through it now he realised he had moved to the left of the saw, it was now slightly to his right. He tried to feel across to his right but his fingers just felt fresh air. With no desire to lay on his side again he tried to jump with his knees.

"Shit," he said out loud as he almost fell forwards off the bench, just throwing his head and shoulders back fast enough to prevent the fall. He opted for a less dramatic way as he shuffled his knees trying to mimic a Michael Jackson dance move with them instead of his feet. It worked, he moved slowly to the right although he rocked a little forwards and back he was in no danger of toppling over.

After three sets of the tiny steps which was all his bound ankles would allow his knees to make he paused and reached behind him, success, or at least partial as his fingers felt the edge of the saw. One more shuffle and he'd be there he thought.

He pushed his right knee along the bench followed by the left,; reaching behind he could almost wrap the fingers of his right hand around the saw blade, but not quite. Leaving his fingers holding the blade he moved his right knee again and instantly regretted it. His knee hit something sharp, it penetrated his jeans and then his flesh. He cried out in anguish and started to fall; despite the pain he reacted quickly enough to push his shoulders and head back ensuring at least he did not topple forwards but with so much movement he lost balance and fell to his right. In desperation he clung to the saw blade as he fell. The saw, its hook, and the other tools all fell with him as the rusty rack came away from the wall. He pitched on to his side, his head making delayed contact with the bench. He bit his own lip for good measure feeling blood run into his mouth and throat. It was but nothing to the feeling in his leg, a damp patch was spreading from his knee, he felt a further pain as something sharp pierced his thigh.

Now in agony he figured rolling off the bench to the floor was no worse than staying where he was. The fall was easy, if short, it was stopping on the ground that hurt. Agony coursed through his body, his head fit to burst, a sudden flash of light in his eyes followed by black.

Eugene came to slowly, as he did he ran a mental check over his body. He thought he had not been out for long the damp patch on his leg was still damp and not congealed so he reckoned either not enough time had passed for that to happen or he was going to bleed to death.

There was so much pain all over his body that he was sure he had not lost too much blood, he had never lost too much blood before but assumed he would feel a lot weaker and light headed. His head was not light, it felt heavy and hurt like hell.

Recovering his senses he wondered for a moment if he should simply give up and go with whatever Andrei and Lena had in store for him. He did not wonder for long. He simply did not trust them to leave him alive.

The blow to the head had affected his night vision slightly, he struggled to make complete sense of where he was; blinking his eyes clear he realised he was facing the bench. He figured the Nissan was behind him. Miraculously the saw was still in his hands but they had been cut, his fingers were sticky with blood. He decided rolling over was not a good idea so he pulled his legs as close to his chest as he could and pressed them down into the ground and pushed, for a short moment they gripped and he moved ahead before they slipped and he remained still. He kept repeating the exercise, his goal the second bench and anything that might help him to keep the blade still enough for him to cut through the ties on his wrists.

With no clear sense of time Eugene could not tell how long it took before his head was touching the bench across the end of the barn. Much of the bleeding had stemmed which at least meant the cuts were not that deep. His right thigh though was in considerable pain, each movement extracting the maximum amount of revenge for him ignoring it's screams for relief. He had no idea what but something was definitely stuck in his leg, more than once he had felt it move, each time the sensation forced bile up his throat. He had worked hard to control the urge to vomit, chocking on his own puke in a barn in the middle of nowhere was not how Eugene Clayton was going to end his life. With each internal scream of agony he brought to mind his father and some of the worst times of his teenage years. The motivation was powerful as he kept saying to himself, "I'll show you, you bastard." He had pushed forwards again.

With the onset of full darkness the clouds of late afternoon had drifted away allowing the moon to provide a surprising amount of additional light. Eugene was relieved that the extra vision would enable him to make some further sense of his surroundings.

Now at the bench he stopped moving and gathered himself. Looking around as much as he could lying on his side. He saw nothing useful, or did he, he thought. "What is that?" he said quietly to himself.

Between the two benches on the ground he could see dark shapes with odd angles, like a model of a cityscape. Pulling his protesting legs back to himself he pushed forwards and managed to gain enough purchase to edge to the right and the gap between the benches. As he did he spotted other odd shapes under the end bench and something that appeared to hang down to the ground. It was almost exactly in line with the shape he had seen earlier on top of the bench. Returning his focus to the items between the benches he inched his way over.

His delight when he saw what was on the ground momentarily overwhelmed the pain he felt as he realised what he was looking at. The dark objects were swage blocks, a kind of die for finishing handmade metal tools. They were almost in his reach.

He pulled his legs up and pushed again, this time he had ended up close to the bench and his feet made contact with something that made a metallic sound, it wasn't the bench. Again he stopped, this time his nose picked up the faint smell of sulphur and ash. He was surrounded by old blacksmith equipment. Defying the pain he moved himself around and gripped the saw in his left hand only as he explored the block for a hole the right size to fit the saw handle. The block was large and he felt dozens of holes and shapes on the edge. Given its size he also knew he would never move it so if he could find the right hole he was certain he could cut the ties.

After several failed efforts to locate the handle he finally managed to insert the handle into a round hole. The saw felt secure. He wriggled himself into a position on his knees again and then through gritted teeth as the pain in his leg threatened to overpower him he rose up and down from the knees his wrists against the saw blade. It worked quicker than he expected and as his hands were freed he flopped forward from the waist bringing his hands to his face and sobbed with relief.

Once again he reached behind him and with the addition of a few more cuts to his hands he freed himself before he turned his attention to his ankle ties. With his ankles free he sat down against the bench in an attempt to settle his ragged breathing. The effort of freeing the ties had brought him to the very edge of exhaustion. "Except, I'm not free," he said, "I'm still locked in here."

Forcing himself to stand and walk he made his way first to the Ford truck, as with his own at home its keys were in the ignition. After all who would try and steal a vehicle out here? He hobbled over to the tractor opened the door and pulled himself up the two metal steps, the tractor key was there to. Could he fire it up and break the door open before getting in the truck and driving off he wondered? Before quickly acknowledging that the idea was stupid at best as the noise of the heavy diesel would bring Andrei to the barn very quickly. Even if the guy was asleep he would be outside the barn by the time he got to trying to leave in the truck.

One decision he did make was to disable the Nissan. He found a metal spike that blacksmiths drove into things like horse shoes to lift them when hot and with the help of a heavy hammer drove a hole in all the tires. With that done he headed to the barn door.

He was only a few feet from it when he heard a noise outside, it sounded like a door opening. He heard it slam shut and then footsteps. He looked around and wondered what was best to do; hide or sit by the tractor and pretend he was still bound? That would be fine unless they came in and put a light on. He ran out of time to think, he heard the padlock being opened and darted towards the tractor as the door was pushed open.

All he heard Andrei say was, "What the fuck..?"

The next sound was the snick click of a weapon being cocked as Andrei saw him. "Stop or I'll shoot," he yelled. Without thinking Eugene dived forwards and threw himself behind the tractor's front loader bucket; as he did a shot rang out, followed by an enormous clang very close to Eugene's left ear. The noise ringing in his head Eugene lay still expecting to hear something further. He heard nothing.

Crawling forward and edging his head passed the other end of the bucket Eugene peered to the left, there was no one there. He pulled himself out and stood up. Just inside the door was a large shape prone on the ground. He walked cautiously over towards Andrei. He was not moving, he lay almost on his side, his right hand out of sight behind him, his left arm somewhere beneath him. Most of his face was gone and the back of his head had been sprayed across the ground and the barn door as the ricocheting bullet had hit him full square in center of the face. Eugene managed not to throw up, he must be getting used to the sight of blood. Then he heard a sound and Lena calling out from the house.

"Andrei, what's going on?"

Eugene did not answer but reached over Andrei's inert body and took the gun from his hand. As he did he heard Lena's footsteps outside. When she stepped through the door at first she could do nothing. Time stopped, her mind confused, frozen briefly like a snowflake headed into a warmer atmosphere, her scream only coming as it thawed. Taking in the gun in Eugene's hand she turned and ran. There was no way Eugene could run fast enough to catch her but he made his way as quickly as he could to the house. Expecting her to be telephoning for help, he was surprised when he heard her voice.

"You killed him," she shouted.

"I didn't, he killed himself. He shot at me and clearly he ain't much used to guns cause the bullet hit the tractor bucket and the ricochet hit him."

Eugene walked towards the door. "Lena, I ain't gonna hurt you, I am coming through the door, okay?" As he went into the building he found her sitting on the floor hugging her knees, great waling sobs of grief coming from deep within her.

With nothing else to do he turned and walked out the door. He made his way over to the GMC van, as he had expected the keys were in the ignition. He took them and made his way to the barn and fired up the Ford. He put on the trucks lights and stood in their glare to examine his leg and hands. His jeans were shredded and his hands looked like pork fat scored for the oven. Since the bleeding had stopped he figured there was nothing else to worry about so pulled himself up into the driver's seat and drove out of the barn.

He was unsure of the road home but with the moon on his left he took the road that kept it there and just headed south.

The Journey Home

With the main lights beginning to dim a spotlight came on and shone brightly on the podium in the centre of a low standing stage to the front. A steady murmur among the gathering slowly faded out with the lights; an air of expectation taking its place.

For a while nothing happened, in fact the time lapse seemed an age and magnified the atmosphere. To the left of the stage a curtain appeared to billow almost as if a wind had erupted, the symbolism was probably intentional as the billowing curtain was followed by a large man attired in a bright grey suit. His shirt was buttoned but he did not wear a tie, his enormous left hand gripped a large book, the size of an encyclopaedia. Without a word he strode to the podium, placed the book on the top and then looked out at his audience. He stared silently, impassive, almost daring someone to break the silence. The first words, though, belonged to the big man. His voice was deep and thundered into life with the heavy rumble of an old Mack truck.

"Beloved, welcome. Welcome. I beseech you to heed my words, I demand that you hear the message I bring for you today. Through life you are either on the road to somewhere or the road to nowhere. Let me be clear, you have a choice…"

The big man's words carried on his voice booming around the place, it sounded like he didn't need the microphone. I was at the back and I knew I was some place, to me the middle of nowhere, but I knew I had come from somewhere.

I had no idea where I was; yesterday I was someplace else. I had no idea where that was either, best I can say is about an hour or two southwest of Chicago. The only reason I was in this gathering was I couldn't find anyone else in the tiny place I had driven into only a few minutes earlier. The place was even smaller than my home town of Grayson. The whole population seemed to be in this building. The building itself was enormous relative to the scale of the town. It must have an identity crisis. A cross between a town hall and place of worship. I wasn't sure if that meant the people in the place were an audience or a congregation. Whatever they were the crowd was mostly black, only a few white faces that I could see, they all seemed enthralled by the speaker.

Certainly the big man on the stage sounded like a preacher so probably they were a congregation. In fact he sounded like one of those tv evangelists, I was just waiting for him to ask everyone to dig deep and give generously to whatever church he was promoting. I'm not a religious guy, I had no idea when I had last been in a church and right now I was beginning to think I shouldn't be in this one. It was hard to tell if the man was just charismatic or as dangerous as an NRA member with a semi automatic. Either way he had his audience entranced with his speaking.

Truth be told he had my attention too, so much so I nearly died of fright when I heard a voice beside me. "Ain't seen you here before."

I looked around and had to look down, I'm no giant but this guy was a midget, least ways he was much smaller than me. I looked at him and clearly he thought I was deaf because he spoke again only with a slightly louder hush. He seemed to want to make sure I heard him but make sure no one else did. "I said, ain't seen you here before." Spelling it out like I was some kind of idiot. Maybe I was standing in this place.

"No sir, you ain't," I replied.

"Well mister, you either brave or plumb stupid," he said, the last word coming out with a double oh sound, before continuing, "this ain't somewhere strangers are welcome."

Oddly I figured this was good news since it was somewhere that obviously meant it weren't nowhere and since I had no idea where I was, maybe I could now find out. All I wanted to do was get home.

I looked at the guy and keeping my voice as hushed as his I asked, "Why?"

"Folk round here worry 'bout strangers. They afraid Reverend big shot gonna punish them," he said pointing at the man on the stage.

"Why would he punish them?"

"That's how he maintains control round here, by fear."

"But you ain't scared are you?"

"No sir I ain't, but then I am a bit unusual round these parts."

My accent I knew was full of southern twang and country language, but this guy sounded like he was from another century. Again I asked him why.

"Well, cos Reverend big shot don't scare me none. I ain't never fallen for his jiggery pokery. See unlike some folk in here I can read and I never seen some the things he say writ in no bible."

As he spoke the man on the stage was winding himself into a frenzy, his voice seeming louder than before, the boom now like that of an airplane going supersonic. The little guy next to me took my sleeve and tugged, nodding his head towards the exit he said, "Mister, best we leave."

Since by now I was not exactly enjoying the performance I saw no reason to object so followed him outside. Once through the doors he kept walking down the sloping lawn to the street. When he reached the street side he pointed at my parked pickup. "That yours?" he asked. When I said yes he simply said. "Well let me in and drive boy, drive."

Like so many in the south he had a musicality to his language. I had narrowed down my whereabouts at least, well to the extent that I must be south of the Mason Dixon line, thereafter I was none the wiser. As we headed away I asked him, "Where to?"

"Just drive, man drive." I'd been promoted at least, boy to man.

"Sure, but I ain't no idea where we are so no idea where to go."

"Just follow this road, I'll tell you when we far enough."

So I drove.

I ended up in the middle of nowhere in a truck I borrowed, some might say I stole. Just a day and half earlier my wrists and ankles had been bound and I was tied to a Massey Ferguson tractor. At one point I was sure I was going to be shot, somehow the idiot with the gun managed to hit the tractor's front loader bucket. The bullet took his own face off before taking off the back of his head. Bad for him, good for me. I had ended up in the mess because of a girl, how else? There's nothing easier to get a single guy to part with his dough than a pretty girl. And Lena, the girl in question, had been pretty, the prettiest girl I had ever met. Then again I hadn't met many.

She was delightful, I was beyond excitement at the prospect of meeting her but then she turned out to be something else altogether. That is her and her friend Andrei did. He was the guy with the gun and now the missing face.

After he managed to kill himself and not me I left Lena in a state of high emotion and drove off in the Ford truck. Having never been anywhere in my life aside from a brief visit to Louisville, Kentucky, I was totally lost. I had no idea where I was. I knew enough about the world to know the moon and the sun rise in the east and I knew having been to Chicago that home was south, so I drove south.

I had driven for a couple of hours with no certainty where I was when I came across a gas station with all its lights on. To begin with I assumed the owner had just forgotten to switch the lights off when turning in for the night. But as I slowed I saw a man walking around inside the shop so I pulled in to the pumps. The gas station guy was as shocked to see me as I was him.

As he stared at me I began to realise why he looked shocked. I wasn't that he had a customer, it was that I looked like I had been in a small war. I had somehow forgotten that my jeans were ripped to shreds and there was blood all over my right leg. My blood. I had also forgotten how painful my hands were. They had also been shredded, partly by holding the serrated blade of a tree saw and partly in my efforts to cut the plastic cuffs from my wrists.

"I don't want no trouble," he said, his step hesitating as he managed to see even more of me in the pool of light spilt from the overheads.

168

I held my hands up as if in surrender and smiled. "Me either," trying to make sure my smile seemed genuine.

"You ain't carryin' are you?"

"No sir, I just want some gas and maybe a map if you got one to sell," I said in reply. I figured a map to be a good idea but I wasn't too sure I could read one. Map reading wasn't something I had learned.

"Gas I can do but no maps here." He seemed to be staring at my legs. "I can do you some work pants too seen as your jeans look all done in," he added, pointing at my right leg. I glanced down, it was the first time I had looked at my leg since getting in the truck. It was a mess. It had not hurt, or at least I had not felt anything until right then.

"There's something sticking out your leg," he said, again pointing. It was only then I noticed a slight glint on my jeans and I moved my hand down to brush it off my jeans and instantly wished I hadn't. I guess if there were any neighbours my howl would have woken them. The sharp pain that shot through my leg and ran all the way up my thigh, over my butt and beyond was like nothing I had felt before. The gas station guy looked horror struck. "Let's leave gassing your truck for now and take a look at that leg," he said turning and walking into the building. I followed him, slowly limping along as though I was the same age as him.

Once inside it was much clearer what was causing the pain. I could see a curved piece of steel sticking out maybe an inch looking for all the world like a metallic curly hair. I made the mistake of touching it again. The metal fragment had passed through my jeans and buried itself in my leg, my thigh was covered in tiny pieces of steel. Memories of being bound and forcing myself along the bench in the barn were nearly as sharply ingrained as the steel. Whatever the barn had once been used for its most recent activities had been working on metal. There had been metal filings all over the place and a lot of them had found their way into me like the sharp teeth of a Piranha. I could also see the gas station guy was much older than I realised, closer to old enough to be my grandfather.

The guy bent down and peered at my leg. "Need to cut that off." He stood up again and walked over to his counter and bent beneath. I heard a few things being shuffled around. When he stood up he had a pair of industrial sized scissors in his hand. Before coming back to me he opened the door of a cupboard and took some things down them came around.

"Son, you best not take offence now but I think we need to get them jeans off and your wounds looked at."

With the adrenalin long gone and the efforts of the night before I was long passed arguing and was now feeling close to exhaustion. He worked like an old seamstress, expertly cutting up the right leg, taking care to go round the piece of metal protruding from me and then peeled away the cloth. He rocked back on his haunches and let out a low whistle.

"I think you've been quite lucky son, seems that metal could easily have caused you to bleed to death."

I looked down and saw the mess for myself. It looked like I had been rolling in glass. As I watched he pulled a pair of reading glasses from his shirt pocket and looked more closely at the metal piece. Without another word he opened the small box next to him and took out a pair of pliers. He looked up at me. He didn't need to say a word. This was going to hurt. And it did, a lot. For the second time that night I howled. But then it was done. He expertly disinfected the whole of my leg, one day he'd make someone a fine nurse I thought. When he was done he put a bandage round the wound and asked to see my hands. Luckily there was no metal stuck in them, just minor cuts all over. He cleaned them too, then went out back. There was a small seat just inside the door and I moved over and sat, the tiredness now beginning to overwhelm me.

When he came back the guy had a neatly folded pair of work pants and a shirt. He handed them to me and said, "Here, take these and get yourself changed, I'll go and gas your truck." The clothes were old ones of his so I didn't need to pay for them. I was too tired to do much else so I lay down on the seat and was unconscious in seconds.

The early signs of dawn had appeared as I was woken by the noise of the door to the store being unlocked. I had not heard him lock me in. He came in carrying coffee and muffins which I devoured in no time. Given that I was trying to find my way home I was not there long. The guy gave me directions to find the interstate, I paid him for the gas and was quickly on my way. I found the I 55 easy enough. The theory was I could follow this all the way to St. Louis, Missouri, and then find the right interstate to get me to Louisville and then head south for Grayson. About an hour after joining the interstate I ran into a detour. To begin with all seemed fine, I was following trucks and other vehicles quite happily. It was maybe an hour later I finally realised the traffic was thin. Somehow I had missed the signs to for the re-route. I drove another two hours and found myself right where I was, plumb in the middle of nowhere.

I never did learn the gas station guy's name but I was grateful for his help.

The drive away from the meeting hall was way longer than I expected. We had been driving for half an hour before I was directed off the road. I turned the truck onto a track into some woods. To begin with the track was quite passable, we could make thirty miles an hour no problem, but then the track started to turn into a mini mountain range and pretty soon we were crawling along. I looked over at the little guy.

"How far we goin'?

"Not far now, nearly there," was the extent of his explanation. He was at least right as a couple of minutes later he directed me to pull into a gap between two trees that nearly took the mirrors of the truck. Everything went dark as we found ourselves enveloped by overhanging trees and thick bushes then, just as quickly as the dark covering, began it opened into a small clearing. The clearing was maybe fifty yards across. To the left hand edge as we approached was a ramshackle building that looked like the kind of den kids would have built. The walls were an odd mix of different types of wood panel, the door didn't appear to match any of the panels and the roof was several sheets of corrugated iron, all of which appeared to be different lengths so over the door way the long piece kind of over hung to form a sort of entrance porch.

"What's this?" I asked him.

"Home," he said. Now I was seriously puzzled, my first thought was if he needed me to give him a ride how had he got into town in the first place. The second was how come he needed to be hidden away like some backwoods survivalist. Not that he could survive much in his tin shack. As I pulled up the guy opened the door and jumped out. He stood in front of the truck and waited for me to join him. I was still moving a lot slower than I would like, my thigh and butt had stiffened like a corpse. As I walked towards him he held out his hand.

"I'm Jimmy, by the way, what do I call you?"

"Eugene," I said, shaking his hand.

"Let's go inside and I'll fix some coffee."

The inside wasn't nearly as bad as the outside. He had a rough kind of kitchen, I could ~~would~~ see a water tower out back but I had no idea what was supplying the power to heat the water. The coffee was pretty good and the seat he showed me to fairly comfortable. But otherwise I was in a world of confusion.

"Jimmy, why did we take off from that meeting or whatever it was?"

"I can't let 'em catch me Eugene, old Reverend big shot thought he got me run off years ago."

"So why'd you go and while we're on the subject how the heck did you get there, it must be fifteen, maybe twenty miles?"

"It's actually 'bout twelve if you know the way through the woods. Takes me around four hours to get there. I go in every week when he gives his sermon to see if I can speak to my wife and Daughter and get 'em to come with me so we can leave this God forsaken hell hole. Been doin' it five years and ain't got to speak to 'em yet."

"Why don't you just go up to them?"

"You don't understand, see the guy I call Reverend big shot, he's no more a priest than me. His name, least he say his name, is Calvin Thomas. He runs the place, calls it his place, refers to the people as his people. Everyone one of them is in fact in servitude, almost slaves. It's right he calls a lot of 'em his people, he fathered most the kids in the place. He is just about the cruellest man you can imagine and he preys on the people's religious faith. Them as don't join in soon disappear. Not sure where but if you don't bend to his rule you don't get far from here. I don't know what he does to 'em but a lot a folk gone missing."

"Slaves, they don't look like slaves to me, besides the guy's black."

"Them's the worst, turn on their own. Not everyone round there is black, he has a few henchmen, one of them is supposedly the Sheriff, but he's appointed by Thomas. He's white and is every bit as cruel as some of them folk you read about, you know them slave overseers. He and his men keep everyone in line. See this guy ain't no idiot. The greatest cruelty of all is everyone has work, they have good homes, they all fed well and they all God fearing so controlling 'em is easy. Most don't know they in servitude. He is one cute sonofabitch."

"So why don't you go and tell the authorities, the Feds maybe?"

"Who'd believe me? Even if I could get them to come, they'd see the clean town, the townsfolk would all say how wonderful life is and that people like me are dead set on ruining their lives. Old big shot helps himself to the women folk, most of 'em seem happy to let him. His henchmen get plenty o'woman too, usually chosen by him. It's hard to tell which of the kids round here were fathered by their mother's husband and which by him. Part of why he hates me is I know my Daughter is mine. I was there both times that mattered and my dear late Ruby lost her life cos o'that low life."

He looked at me curiously, as though he wanted to check if I believed him or not. I wasn't sure what to believe. The first thing that I struggled with was how he survived in this place. I could see where he got his water but he clearly had power and that was harder to make sense of. Without being sure of this I could not be sure whether to believe him or not. So I asked him.

He chuckled as he replied. "Come out back." I followed him through the rear door and got one's curiosity satisfied instantly. Right out the back door was a well cared for and cultivated piece of land. The property far from being on the edge of the clearing was actually only about two thirds the way across. He had plenty food growing out here, potatoes and vegetables a plenty. He turned to the right and as we got to his little water tower I could see chicken wire. He had a half a dozen hens so eggs were in ready supply. There was a little hen house at the rear of the run and behind it a small shed. We walked to the shed and he pulled the door open. Hanging from the roof beams was a deer carcass, in the corner was some fishing gear, he seemed to have it all covered.

"As you can see," he said, holding his arms wide, "I ain't starved, though I do confess I don't always stick to the seasons when it comes to huntin'."

"What about the power?"

Once again he walked away, this time out of the shed and to the back door of the property. What I had not seen when we stepped out earlier was a low level cupboard, a bit like an old coal bunker. Inside were six twelve volt batteries. "Follow me and I'll show you how I charge 'em."

Yet again he walked off without waiting for me to respond, only this time we walked down the centre of his vegetable garden. The bushes at the back seemed even denser than the ones we had come through earlier, the trees were more sparse so more light came through, the garden was facing south so had plenty of sun. I had no clue where we could be going as when we drew closer to the bushes they seemed even more thick than I had thought. He took two steps to the right when we reached the bushes and stepped between two of them, he disappeared instantly. I had to duck down to follow him and I could see there was a narrow gap through. It was no more than about ten yards long, when we passed through I could see yet another clearing, this one much smaller than where his home was. Just large enough for a tiny shed and what I figured was a late 1980's Dodge RAM pickup. I was astonished, maybe Jimmy would make a better survivalist than I had thought.

The truck's flatbed had four five gallon gas cans on it. There were five more in the little shed alongside an old generator. "I charge me the batteries with this," he said pointing at the generator. I use the truck to go to a gas station and get out to the road south to Bladon. Takes me an hour just to get out to the road, the track is rough and I can only manage about walking speed. Bladon's just over thirty miles away. I do some bits of work down there for a few folk, driving, manual work, anything that goes really. Folk down there think I live close by but they all keeps themselves to themselves so no one gets too nosy. I keep looking for someone to ask for help but ain't found anyone yet. 'Till now that is."

"What do you mean 'till now?" I asked.

"Eugene, you gotta help me," he said, help without sounding the L, a bit like BB King singing Help the Poor.

"Jimmy, I can't help you, you need the police or the Feds."

"I told you, they ain't ~~gone~~ gonna pay no never mind to a guy like me. No I gotta take Corrine myself somehow. I gotta do it soon Eugene, before he start to think time is right for her to be in his bed." Jimmy's voice started to crack, his eyes had become moist. All the confidence he had displayed by showing me his carefully crafted private world gone. Shattered with the terrible thoughts of what might happened to his daughter.

"How old is she?"

"Just turned fifteen."

I felt a lump in my throat. Living in Grayson County does not prepare you for some of life's worst things. Aside from the events of last year Grayson had mostly gone unharmed by the evils of the wider world for as long as I could remember.

"So what am I supposed to do?" I asked him.

"Well I figure we can go into town next week when they all in the hall. I can point Corrine out to you when they go in and you wait and take her when they come out."

"Whoa, Jimmy. Firstly you said they won't take kindly to seeing strangers about so I can hardly just sit in the street unnoticed. And second they ain't going to just let me drive away with Corrine, she might not want to come in any case. Kidnapping is a Federal crime you know."

He stared hard at me for a few moments. The sadness in his eyes betraying how he really felt. He sighed and put his hands to his head. "I guess you right

Eugene, that's not the best thought out plan. But we gotta do somethin'."

We spent the next couple of hours coming up with one not so clever idea after another. All of them too stupid to talk about. Eventually as afternoon turned to evening Jimmy suggested fixing something to eat. As I had not eaten all day I was very hungry, if a little suspicious about what he might serve up.

I was pleasantly surprised, although he didn't serve any fries we ate a spicy chicken with rice. Even Harry would be proud of that. Harry's Chicken and Rib shack was my favourite place to eat in Grayson. In fact it was about the only place I ate, my microwave tv dinners don't really count as food. We drank more coffee and went back to trying to make a plan to rescue his daughter. I still had doubts she would even want to leave.

Jimmy had not seen his daughter for five years, best he could remember she had been nine years old at the time. Up until the death of his wife Jimmy had been happy enough to put up with life under the yoke of Calvin Thomas. For a while he had even quite enjoyed it he said. They lived in a small single storey, right next door to Ruby's sister Violet and her kids. Her old man had died the year Corrine was born, apparently an accident at work. When it happened no one questioned the facts.

Things seemed pretty good all in all, they were all well housed, had jobs, the money they made wasn't huge but they needed nothing. Their families had pretty much all come from parts of the south where being poor was expected. Starving half the time seemed the norm. So where they were now was idyllic in comparison.

Jimmy was fifty two years of age and as such was born during segregation. When he was brought up his parents still thought white folk were entitled to be called sir and m'am just because of the colour of their skin. Taking separate buses and being in different schools was just the way it was. Jimmy saw the world a little differently. Heavily influenced by the civil rights movement and Martin Luther King who saw to it that those differences were changed. Though some say even now things are not that much better. But from where he was at birth to where he was when his daughter was born might as well have been another planet. Jimmy was a happy man.

Things changed after his daughter's birth he explained. Suddenly with something to be responsible for he began to see things around the place he had barely noticed before. Or maybe it was marrying late and having a family when most folk have got teenagers.

Either way life was too peaceful. So peaceful he figured something weren't right.

He first questioned the goings on in McGovern when a guy at work got into minor argument with his supervisor. It was nothing really. It was a hot day and they were loading bags of rice onto pallets by hand, he dropped one and it split. The supervisor yelled at him, Jimmy said he thought the supervisor's reaction was nuts. Eventually another supervisor came along and all three went off. Jimmy never saw the guy again. I realised when he mentioned the name McGovern it was the first time I had heard the name of the place.

He spoke to Ruby and her sister about it on the porch that evening as they swung on the seat sipping Ruby's homemade lemonade. The women had clearly not been as blind as him as they recalled a number of similar events over the last few years. Jimmy had begun to pay a bit more attention and soon wondered how free their lives were. Unlike his grandparents he was fed well, he had work but nothing else. They got up every morning, tended chores, went to work, got home, more chores and church on Sunday. At work he realised some of the supervisors simply stood and watched. They changed around so they did not have the same man watching every day. But that was all they did, watch.

Every now and again Calvin Thomas would visit where he worked. The supervisors became nervous and slightly more aggressive towards the men. The place had to be spotless so they would stop whatever they were doing and sweep, polish and shine stuff to the point where everything looked like it was new.

Jimmy first got into trouble when he asked if he could go on one of the delivery runs with the truck. He asked his supervisor who took him to his boss and there he was told that only chosen ones went on the trucks. Obviously he asked how he could be chosen and who chose. Only Reverend Thomas could decide that he was told. It was then he realised he had never even spoken to the man, so he decided he would.

Calvin Thomas made no secret of where he was most days, he had a small office next to his church. Jimmy's request was not met with much enthusiasm. Thomas was polite but firm telling him he needed to spend more time in church and doing Gods good deeds before he could be considered. It was following that visit he started to notice two men in particular paying him a lot of attention. Taking turns to follow him, sit in a car a short way from their house and just watch. This went on for several months. Not being easy to intimidate he went and saw Thomas again. This time he was told to wait in the office and Thomas left the room. When the door opened it was not the Reverend who walked in but the Sheriff and one of his deputies. They took Jimmy around the back of the building and beat him with their batons, taking care not to hit his face. As he lay exhausted and in pain they told him he needed to get back in line and know his place or worse would follow.

For a while it worked. Jimmy went about his daily life keeping within the rules, he even lied to Ruby about what happened to him. Things really turned bad when one night struggling to sleep he made his way onto the front porch. He was sitting in his favourite chair in the corner, there was little moonlight and he was unseen. He'd been there only a few minutes when the Reverend's car pulled up outside his sister in law's house. He saw the big man get out and walk to her front door, also in the car was the Sheriff, he got out and leant on the car.

A short while later Jimmy heard a scream from next door and went across to see what was going on. Without thinking he ran in through the back door, he could hear a mix of cries and grunts as he made his way across the kitchen. His hand was on the door handle to the passage but he never got to open it.

The blow that struck him laid him out flat. In his desire to get to the cause of the scream Jimmy had not seen or heard the Sheriff follow him into the building.

Throughout the next day Jimmy was severely beaten and left with a clear message ringing in his ears. Either he stepped back into line or his family would be minus a man in the house.

At Ruby's insistence Jimmy got his head down and towed the line. She was happy with life in McGovern, they had a child and she weren't going to let him mess things up she told him so he did as he was told. Things changed when Ruby took sick and died. It all happened quickly, she started to complain of stomach problems which she and her sister Violet tried to treat with potions and old folk remedies but nothing worked.

McGovern did not have a doctor let alone a hospital so eventually one of the Reverend's people came, he was usually the one that saw to it a doctor was brought in if needed. By the time one came Ruby was bed ridden and in complete agony. The cancerous lump in her stomach now so huge the swelling could be seen. With nothing to do for her the doctor gave her pain relief and she passed her final days asleep or in severe pain, oblivious to the world around her.. Jimmy thought it a blessing when she died, he also thought the doctor had not been called because of who Ruby was married to.

Violet took Corinne in to care for her and Jimmy vowed to end the Reverend's rule. His big mistake was telling the man himself. He was lucky the Sheriff and his gang were not around when he confronted the Reverend. The big man never got his own hands dirty but the threat was clear. Time for Jimmy to get out of McGovern or die.

When he got home he loaded his Dodge pickup with everything he thought he might need and left in a hurry.

By the time Jimmy had finished telling me how he came to be where he was I was committed to help and if I could bring the whole thing to an end.

Since we could not come up with a workable plan Jimmy suggested we go to McGovern that night so he could show me how he got in and out without anyone knowing. We figured it would be a good idea to scout the place and see if any ideas came to us as a result.

Jimmy had the eyesight of an owl as he worked his way up a trail he had been on a hundreds of times. In the dark and with me slowing things down it took us closer to five hours than four to make it to the edge of McGovern. By the time we reached the church, which I still figured looked like a huge town hall, it was 2am. The building was close to the trees and the last fifty yards the trees had been thick undergrowth providing ideal cover even if we had walked up in the daylight. Further visual protection was provided by a line of fancy shrubs that were around the church in a horseshoe shape the open side to the road that I had parked in earlier that day when I had wandered into the mid week service. A service I now knew the whole population of McGovern had to attend. Which is why no one had seen me arrive.

We stopped at the row of bushes and Jimmy beckoned me to kneel beside me. Speaking in hushed tones he said. "See it's quite easy to ~~you~~ get here undetected." I nodded in agreement. I doubt he could see it to well but he seemed happy enough as he carried on speaking.

"Thomas's office is over yonder," he said pointing to the far left corner of the rear of the building as we looked at it. We had a clear view to the right side of the building and out into the street. The moonlight being bright we got a decent view of things even though I could not make all the dark shapes out properly.

"Across the street is the Sheriff's office and he lives in the house at the back of it. The rest of the properties on that side of the street are those of Reverend big shot's chosen men. If you could see past the shrubs to the right you would see the road continues straight, that's the way we left in your truck. There's only one road off it, to the left. That's where my old place was and where Violet lives. There are two streets off to the left of it and everyone of the residents lives on one them streets. Last time I counted the whole place has around two hundred folk here including Thomas and his men. Beyond the streets with the houses on it the road runs to the farm buildings. Them's where I worked. As best I can make out Calvin Thomas has had the farm for a good long time and he created the first buildings to house farm workers. Then somewhere along the line he came up with the idea of creating McGovern. Since I got outta here I can see it's like some kinda of-cult. Manipulated and driven to serve him and him only. I'm not sure what he does to keep his gang onside but it sure works. The way he behaves I figure it won't be long that most of the people here under the age of fifteen will be his offspring. He takes whichever woman he wants now. Any man objects he is likely to have a problem breathing real quick. When we first came it weren't so bad but bit by bit it got worse. Based on what I see now when I come here is the number of young children is growing and growing quick. I see mothers and kids themselves carry babies into church on a Sunday. I don't normally come here for his mid week service so you were just lucky I saw you at the back. If anyone had turned and seen you in the door way... Well, I doubt you would have been popular."

"So what do we do now?" I asked.

"Ain't sure but I reckon we could go over towards Violet's place so you can see how things look."

We made our way through the bushes and on to the lawn. Keeping tight to the shrubs we got down to the street and once again Jimmy stopped and crouched down. As we did the moonlight started to fade with an encroaching cloud. I looked up and realised it would soon be very dark.

From where we crouched we could make out the buildings across the street and along its entire length. From my visit earlier I had not noticed just how small the place really was. I could just make out the road leading away from the main street as Jimmy had described. Seeing this tiny place so peaceful like this it was hard to believe a word Jimmy had said. I was also struggling to understand why we could not just drive in here collect Corrine and leave. The only problem I could envisage was she might not want to go.

"Why don't we cross the street and go see the lay of the land by Violet's place?" I asked.

"Sure, but let's just wait a few minutes, you never know someone might be about." Now I really did think he was maybe a little crazy or had been watching to many old war movies. There was nothing but stillness. Instead of objecting I figured best to go along with him and said, "Ok."

It seemed to me we waited forever, it had become very dark, the properties across the street now just dark shapes.

"Since this side of the street is open I figure we should cross and walk along the other side, that way we'll be less easy to see," he said.

I tapped his shoulder and grunted acknowledgement. As if I had pressed a start button he stood and looked round at me, I stood with him and we ran across the street. We weren't halfway when we regretted even moving.

As if by magic the street was suddenly full of light, like a baseball park all lighted up for a night game. I was instantly dazzled, blinded almost. If we had not both stopped I am sure I would have fallen as I lost all sense of where I was and which way was up. Seconds later we heard a heavy engine moving rapidly through the gears headed our way.

Like blind rats in a sewer we turned and ran, or rather stumbled rapidly back the way we had come. Diving full length like a batter headed for the home plate we hit the ground behind the first shrub in the row beside the church. As we did the engine noise turned to a screech of rubber.

We didn't stop to look at first. Jimmy just carried on scuttling forwards and I crawled rapidly behind him. After getting back beyond the shrubs and into the thickest part of the bushes he stopped. For a moment we lay there catching our breath. It seemed we had at least got this far without detection.

I rolled over on to my front and crawled forward and got to a point where I could see back alongside the church and some of the street, the bright lights making sure I could see plenty. The car that had arrived was mostly obscured by the shrubs but the guy with the gun in his hand wasn't. He was walking along the line of the buildings across the street looking to his left every other stride as he moved quite rapidly, presumably looking for whatever had set the lights off. As he drew closer to the Sheriff's place a light went on in a front room swiftly followed by a door opening. The Sheriff stood there also with a gun in his hand, the only difference being his was a hand gun. The other guy seemed to be holding a rifle or maybe a twelve gauge. It was hard to tell from where I was.

Pulling myself backwards just in case they could see me I rolled back over and crawled to where Jimmy was waiting.

"Shit, I knew the guy was nuts but he's got the place staked out like a jail," Jimmy said. "Best we get away from here, I don't think they seen us but let's not hang about."

We stayed low until we were well into the trees. No lights had picked us out so we stood and headed back the way we ~~had~~ came in. The walk back was tiring, it seemed to take forever, my body was far from recovered from its recent battles so by the time we got back to Jimmy's place I was exhausted. Dawn had broken whilst we made our way back so at least visibility had not been a problem.

There was only one bed in his home so Jimmy got me a roll of blankets and I made myself comfortable on the floor. It didn't matter, I could have slept anywhere.

It was late afternoon when I woke, Jimmy was nowhere to be seen. I rolled his blankets up and left them on his bed and went outside to find him. He wasn't tending his garden and I couldn't see him over by his chickens so I went through the trees out back.

He was busy with the generator and was surrounded by his gas cans. His hearing was as good as his eyesight and he was already looking towards the gap in the trees that I appeared through.

"You sleep long," he said in greeting.

"Um, I've had a crazy coupla days," I said. I leant on the hood of his pickup and wished I hadn't. It was as hot as hell. I stepped back with slight yelp. "You been out?" I asked a bit unnecessarily as the only way his hood could be that hot was if he had driven the pickup some place.

"Needed some gas," he said pointing at the cans.

He stopped what he was doing and wiped his hands on his pants, "Coffee?"

I nodded a reply, my mouth still not fully awake. So we walked back to his home, I struggled to call it a house. I sat at his little table while he busied himself making coffee. It might not have been the best I had ever had but right then it certainly tasted the best. We sat in silence for quite some time before I asked what he thought we should do. His expression was a picture of misery.

"I ain't sure, thought of nothing else all day and I just feel even more helpless now than I did before."

Maybe because of the way I was brought up I had no understanding of emotion. But something touched me and for maybe the first time in my life I was feeling genuinely sorry for someone. I felt pretty helpless to.

Thinking through the issues I realised even if we could come up with a plausible way of getting to Violet's house we had no way of telling if Jimmy's daughter would come with us. If she refused were we supposed to just take her anyway? To me that seemed plain stupid but leaving her at the mercy of Thomas was less appealing than a jail term for kidnap.

"Is there another way into the place other than the through road and the walk we took last night?" I asked him.

"Only other way in would be across the farmland I guess. Not real sure how to get there without being seen or ending up in a ditch someplace."

"We should look though, be stupid to just give in now," I said.

"Thing is Eugene, a lot of that land is wet, real wet, they grow rice there. I never worked on the land I was just in the sheds working machines, packing and driving a forklift truck. They got plenty of tracks between the fields and such, just I don't know any of it. We can't go in the daytime, we'll be seen for sure and at night as I say we could easily do somethin dumb."

He sounded more and more miserable as he spoke.

"Well we can't sit here and do nothing," I said. "Think of Corinne and what might happen if we don't get her away from there. I figure we should drive around there and see if we can find a place to get onto the farm whilst its daylight. We can then make a plan to go back at night. Thomas ~~might'a~~ mighta had the street all lighted up like Fort Knox but I bet he ain't got the land set up the same way."

Maybe it was my positive tone or perhaps the realisation that quitting would leave Corinne to the mercy of Thomas, I don't know, but either way he looked a little brighter. We agreed to go now and to take the Ford as it was the right side of the forest and neither of us was worried if it were lost. First Jimmy retrieved a map from his Dodge and we set off. The forest was a clear break in the land, to the south and west of the forest the layout of the area was more old fashioned, some of the roads had bends in them and the fields we not perfectly squared off. On the McGovern side it was laid out like a grid. We decided not to risk taking one of the tracks that led into the land as we drove south east but to take the first metalled road east Jimmy had seen on the map. I thought we would never reach it, after the longest half hour I had known Jimmy told me to take it slow, at speed it would have been easy to miss the four-way intersection. With no signs I had no idea where any road led but we made a left and carried on driving for twenty minutes before anyone spoke. It was me who broke the silence.

"Jimmy, we must have come sixty miles in all, we have to be so far away from McGovern we will need an airplane to get there."

"You're right but we have taken the first two metalled roads we came to. We could have gone back towards McGovern before trying to get round the back and maybe I have been too careful but I know the roads closer to McGovern can be seen from the land so this way we can get directly round back. The farm lies almost exactly east to west. At the west end of the place is where all the buildings and houses are. There are two clear tracks parallel to each other that come into the place from the east. I ain't no idea where they are but I figure we can find 'em. This road intersects with the road immediately to the south of the farm. I reckon if we go beyond that intersection we should find a track onto the place."

I just grunted acknowledgement and drove. He was right though, nearly an hour later we hit the road that led back to McGovern. I pulled in just beyond it.

"Now what?" I asked him.

"Ain't too sure, maybe we just find a likely track on from here and see where we get."

"Yup, sounds as good a scheme as any I can think of," I said putting the truck in gear and pressing down on the gas pedal. We did not have far to go before we saw a track on the left that looked just fine for the Ford to handle. What neither of us knew was whether it went where we wanted. I'd asked Jimmy earlier about the size of the farm and he had no clue so we just drove in hope.

The first twenty minutes was easy going, I bet the dust we threw up could be seen halfway to St. Louis but we just kept going. Although the truck was bounced around all over the place most of the time ~~sometimes~~ I was able to keep to around forty most of the time. Then things started to slow, the first thing was a rickety looking bridge over an irrigation channel. I pulled up and we both went to look at it. I looked to our right and left to see if an alternative might be visible but could see nothing. We walked over it and although there were a few rotten looking planks down the center the main cross beams seemed pretty strong and the parts the truck wheels would touch had obviously been patched a time or two so we figured it was safe. Just to be sure I drove over alone and left Jimmy to watch. I had no idea if he would be able to get me out if the thing had collapsed, putting me and the truck in the water, but luckily I didn't find out. With me safe on the other side Jimmy jogged over and climbed back in.

The track on the other side was rougher than the first stretch so we struggled to get to twenty miles an hour. There was plenty of water around to, but the fields the track bisected had no crop of any sort in them. They were brown and almost arid looking, a weird contrast given the water that ran in the ditches around the place.

After about fifteen minutes we hit an impossible challenge, a ten foot high wire mesh fence. Clearly we had found the back of the farm but like the town of McGovern it was clearly not somewhere for strangers to visit. The only break in the fence was directly in front of us, a padlocked gate.

"Shit," I said, pulling to a stop and taking the truck out of gear. Jimmy echoed my sentiment and we looked at each other, that forlorn look reappearing on his face.

Without a word we both got out and walked to the gate. The lock was on the other side but I figured a good set of bolt cutters would take the chain no problem. The problem was we had no bolt cutters. We talked about coming back with cutters to get in, as we did I glanced at my watch and said, "It'll be dark when we get back."

"I know, but maybe dark is best."

I had thought about this all the way from him his place and come to the conclusion our only choice was going to be to get as close to McGovern as we could in day light and then try to get Corinne out under cover of darkness. I figured that was going to be tough on its own without the taking on the track in the dark, now we were contemplating doing the drive twice in the dark.

I looked up and down the length of the fence, to my left and roughly south there was nothing to see but fields. To my right and to the north there was at least some break in the land I could not make out well enough if there was anything else but there were trees for sure about a mile, maybe a little more in that direction. There was no way of telling whether there were any ditches or such to impede us but I was sure we could drive the Ford along the fence line. An idea was beginning to take shape in my head. I climbed on the back of the truck and stared into the farm, I couldn't see anything.

Climbing back off I told Jimmy my plan. He looked at me and grinned, patting me on the arm he said, "Let's go."

Right now he was about as desperate to get his daughter as could be imagined and I am sure he would have been pleased with any plan. I didn't think much to mine but it was the only one we had so we got back in the pickup and drove.

The drive was easy enough and fortunately no ditches. We got to the trees and I pulled the truck up with the trees, hiding it from anyone looking from the direction of the farm. I figured we had now come as far as we could in total daylight so whatever we did next was likely to be done in fading light and then darkness. We went to the trees, now we were there they stood a lot higher than I realised. The trees were native bur oaks and the two closest to the fence towered over it at around thirty or forty feet. They had branches to match. Standing at the fence I looked up at the nearest and a smile came over my face.

I looked at Jimmy and pointed to the tree and said, "I can shin up that easy. That branch looks strong enough to get me over the fence, just prey I don't bust something dropping down. When I'm over drive back to the gate and wait for me there."

Scaling such a mature tree was a synch, I just needed a boost from Jimmy to get hold on the lowest branch and I was quickly out of site. A few minutes later I inched out on the branch, as I got closer to the fence I could tell it only just made it beyond the fence line and I figured I might catch the fence on the way over. I just hoped the paranoid Reverend had not electrified it. Fortunately he hadn't.

Twenty minutes later we were back at the fence and Jimmy recovered the ugly looking Magnum revolver from the truck's cab. I had meant to throw the dam thing away but simply hadn't found anywhere sensible after I took the truck. Taking hold of it by the barrel he passed it into me and then stepped well away from the fence. I cocked the weapon and preyed I did not do an Andrei and shoot myself. The round took the lock off with ease. The chances of anyone hearing the loud thunder of the weapon was remote and in these parts even if they had they would probably think nothing of it.

Opening the gates to let Jimmy in I had a sudden panic attack, what if they were alarmed? With no time to worry I pushed them shut and ran the chain through the handles to keep them closed. Jimmy shuffled over to the passenger seat and I climbed in and drove us onwards. Whether it was a wise idea or not we had pretty much abandoned my earlier worry that going onto the place in daylight would get us seen.

We were moving much slower now and kicking up a lot less dust. We passed the occasional clump of bushes beside the track. The track itself ran parallel to a ditch, I had no clue if we were set to find another in our way. By now we were driving past cultivated land and the risks of being seen were increasing so it was a blessing that the light was fading fast. I had to keep slowing as it did and within no time at all we were only making walking speed. The temptation to put the lights on was huge but with our eyes adjusting to the dark we just kept going.

The first signs that we had made it to the farm was oddly shaped dark patches to the front and off to our right. The shapes becoming more clearly defined rectangles as we got closer. We were maybe a half a mile away when Jimmy put his hand on my left arm and said, "Stop."

I did as I was told and looked at him expecting an explanation but instead he was staring intently into the distance.

"We need to stay on this track a piece. I think we can get right up in line with the end barn and leave the truck there," he said pointing in the distance. What he was pointing at I had no idea, I could see nothing. I put the truck back in gear and we eased forwards again. Ten minutes later we pulled to a stop tight against the southern wall of a barn. I'd assumed there would be no security lights at the back of the place but it was only now that we had got this far I could breathe a little easier.

The truck was facing the area of the housing with the bulk of the farm off to our right. We left the truck and moved to the end of the barn furthest away from the housing to check around the back. As at the end of last night it was very dark under a cloudy sky. My night vision was thankfully fully attuned and I had Jimmy and his experienced night sight for good measure. We peered round the back of the barn, nothing to see so we made our way along the back. The far corner opened into a yard large enough for eighteen wheelers to get in and manoeuvre to the huge silo's across from the barn. Beyond them Jimmy told me were a variety of sheds and the farm offices.

We waited at the corner for a few moments, I looked up and stared hard just beneath the guttering at the gable end. I couldn't see a magic eye for the security system. It's where I would have put one. Relieved there was nothing there we took a tentative step out into the open. The area was a good fifty yards across and was open all the way to the street to the western end where the housing was.

When we reached the silos I stopped and looked back. On the front end of the barn we had left I could see a small square shape. I could not be sure but I figured it was a floodlight. It was no surprise the area had lights, all we had to hope was they weren't connected to an automatic system.

The sheds beyond the silos were close, no more than ten yards. We went across and looked round the outsides. The end closest to the land had windows.

"That's the office," Jimmy said. "The rest of this shed has the store and the farm equipment. The packing sheds are the set beyond this."

"Ok," I said trying a door handle. It was locked. Whilst it was no great shock it was frustrating, I was keen to see what we could find that could help with any contingency. Since a robbery was probably not something Calvin Thomas feared I took off a boot and bust in a window. Once it was opened I gave Jimmy a boost to let him climb up, open the window and clamber through and , once he was in he ran over to open the door. The office was a large open area, there was were a couple of desks and a load of cabinets. One thing that struck me as odd was there was only one telephone. Halfway along the left hand wall was a door. I walked over to try it, the door was not locked. Beyond it was a windowless area. I would have loved a torch, I could have turned a light on, no one outside would see but it would also mean my night vision was wrecked. Leaving the door open I went inside and stood still for a moment. The area was full of shelf stacks. I went to the one nearest the door and felt around the bottom shelf. My hand hit something plastic about two feet high and six inches across. On top was a handle and a large screw top. I tugged it out and pulled it into the office and looked at the label. Satisfied even in that light it was what I had expected to find I put the container back and closed the door. Walking around the office I gathered the waste paper bins and as much other paper as I could find and piled it against the wooden door.

I checked my handy work and then we left.

Back at the truck I let Jimmy take the lead as we made our way across some relatively rough land with thick grass growing from it. The land ran up the back of his old house about a quarter of a mile from the farm.

Jimmy's old place was the second property we came to, like the others it was fully dark. We paused on the back porch before taking the next steps of our plan.

We ran across the short open space between the two properties and at an identical back porch to Jimmy's we stopped briefly. Jimmy slowly turned the handle and pushed. The door opened, unlike the Reverend the other residents of McGovern had no fear of a break in or a break out. The door opened into a narrow hall that ran to the front. There was a small kitchen to our left and the two bedrooms were on our right, the living room was at the front on the left as we looked.

Jimmy figured he should wake Violet and explain what we were doing but he didn't know for sure which was her room. We stood still for a moment and then Jimmy tiptoed down the corridor having decided the front room was most likely. I followed closely and I guess that's why I never saw the kitchen door open and the tiny strip of light. Nor did I hear anything until I felt a blow, more like a heavy sting really on the back of my head. If it was meant to incapacitate me the blow was a failure but it did succeed in making me yelp ad and stumble slightly. As I turned to see what had hit me I saw the tiniest woman I had seen in years. She screamed some obscenity at me but before she could hit me again Jimmy pushed past and grabbed hold of the woman.

"Violet stop! It's me, Jimmy, we're here to help you is all," he said.

The woman was clearly stunned even in the poor light, I could see her mouth fall open. Recovering slightly she said, "Jimmy that really you?"

"Yup, its me." With that she started to cry and hung on to Jimmy as though her life depended on it, which it probably did but she couldn't know that. The commotion in the hall had brought the other occupants of the house into the hall. All three girls were slightly taller than Violet, one of them was Corrine, but which I had no idea.

What followed was chaotic. First Corrine refused to believe Jimmy was her father and she seemed terrified of me. So she just screamed. The other girls just started babbling a high level of panic in their voices. Violet eventually managed to hush them up for fear of bringing attention to the place. She ushered all of us into the tiny kitchen, it was a tight squeeze.

With the girls quiet Jimmy explained he had come to take them away from the place. After telling them why I was here with him and how we had got there the room went silent. For a while no one even moved, I worried they would not want to leave. Then finally Violet spoke.

"Thank the lord Jimmy. That evil man was going to get here sooner or later for the girls. Both Annie and Corrine are old enough to know what's going on and old enough for his eye to fall this way," she said.

Shooing the girls out to get dressed Violet turned to Jimmy a tear in her eye. "Where you been Jimmy? I thought you must be dead by now since you never came back."

"Violet I been trying to get you away."

"Well just as well you come, cos the Reverend ain't interested in old flesh like me no more, he be down for them girls soon enough." She spat the last words out.

A heap of questions came into my mind but none of it was my business and we sure didn't have the time. "Jimmy we need to get out of here." He nodded his head and pushed Violet to the door. She took the direction and quickly shuttled down to her room.

Five minutes later Violet and the three girls were standing in the hall. All six of us then headed out and made our way back to the pickup. Thankfully the truck had a crew cab so fitting us all in would be no trouble. If we could there that is. As we stepped back out the door I could see the lights in Jimmy's old place were on.

"Shit, looks like trouble," I said.

Jimmy pushed the women back inside and stood beside me. We watched for a few minutes and aside for a shadow moving inside we saw no one. Then the light went out. That's when we noticed the Sheriff's car parked out front. Violet appeared at Jimmy's elbow and spoke.

"They moved a young woman in there after Jimmy run and she is popular with the sSheriff, he visits two times a week at least. She's so far under their spell she has no clue what's going on. More and more folk like that round here now. Should be safe to go now if the lights out."

I nodded agreement and Violet went and fetched the girls and we headed away from the property at right angles to where we wanted with Jimmy leading. We figured the further into the grass we went the better. We got back to the truck without any more problems.

Once there I took the revolver out of the glovebox and the box of Diamond matches I had found in the truck.

Although we had made it to the truck without discovery Jimmy and I figured we should cause a large enough distraction to cover our tracks. We headed back to the store.

I had one further idea before setting the place alight, I picked up the telephone. I could only remember two telephone numbers, Pete Gill's and my own. I dialled the latter and when my phone was answered I asked the guy tending my place for what I needed. I hung on a minute while he got what I wanted. When I hung up I immediately re dialled, I was not surprised my call went straight to a voicemail. I left Agent James Ralston of the FBI a short message. His was the only business card I had ever been given, that I had kept it,struck me as strange.

Setting the fire was a synch. I made sure the heap of paper and the cloth from the wooden chairs I'd piled on it were well ablaze before Jimmy and I went back to the truck.

Starting the motor was nerve wracking, having the women now made the whole thing a lot more scary. I wound the window down but heard nothing other than the low rumble of the truck engine. I reversed quietly around the corner and we were instantly bathed in light.

"Shit," I said out loud. Somehow Jimmy and I had walked back and forth between the buildings without triggering a light. We had not even seen a sensor but clearly we had missed one. An alarm struck up at the same time sounding like the kind warning used for a nuclear fallout. I stopped the truck and got out with the gun in my hand.

"Jimmy you drive, I'll get on the back." Not waiting for an answer I leapt into the trucks flatbed and banged on the roof. Jimmy hit the gas with the trucks lights on we sped away. Maybe I'd seen too many cops shows but I felt sure someone would soon be after us. I was wrong, but then again right.

Before we had travelled fifty yards bright headlights struck us from the left. Something was moving fast out of the farm yard. It was hard to tell but I was sure it was the Sheriff. The pickup was bouncing all over the place and I was struggling to keep still in the back so focussing on the vehicle producing the lights was difficult. I had no idea what to do, getting away was probably impossible. Even if Jimmy could pin the gas pedal to the floor we had only one way to go so even an idiot could follow. I figured I needed to deter the vehicle or even stop it. I had the magnum but using that I was as likely to hit the moon as the automobile. I was thinking hard for an idea when the biggest heavy, whooshing, whump sound I had ever heard rolled over us like a huge wave of surf hitting the beach. The fire had hit the chemicals and fertiliser. Looking at the shed I saw a huge ball of flame leap into the night sky the sight was both terrifying and wonderful. The noise was so extraordinary it caused Jimmy to stop. As he looked through the rear window at me I realised my chance, I looked back at the pursuing vehicle. It too had stopped. Raising the gun and aiming just beneath the left headlight I fired a shot at what I hoped was the tire. I lowered my aim a fraction and took another shot. I did the same to the right. With four rounds spent I had used all the ammunition we had. The ring in my ears from the weapon was almost debilitating. I turned back to the cab and banged the roof. Jimmy got the message and gunned the motor. I've no idea if I had hit anything but the vehicle behind was not pursuing.

Looking back as we bounced and plummeted our way east on the track the sky over McGovern now brightly lit, the distraction we'd caused had turned out to be monumental. I figured right now Thomas and his cronies would not be worrying too much about how it started but figuring ways to stop it. Falling over in the back yet again I banged on the cab roof and Jimmy brought the pickup to a halt. I climbed down, there was no need to worry if anyone was coming as they weren't. I tossed the magnum into the ditch, with no bullets it was of no use.

I got into the passenger side of the truck and Jimmy set off again at a more sedate pace;   we were home free.

Stephen Harper's Gift

Like so many other people Stephen Harper had joked about robbing a bank when his finances ran short. He never actually imagined that one day he actually would do it, but that is what he had done. Perhaps more surprisingly his finances had not run short. Now as he stared out of the window of his short term rental in a tiny hamlet, near to Port Vendres in the far south west of France, he began to reflect on what had happened and what was to come. He could not control of what was now likely to happen beyond his own actions but he decided this was not something he should worry about.

A few days earlier following months of planning and preparation Stephen had robbed a branch of the Central Counties Bank in a small northern English town. He had chosen the branch well; although a small branch in an equally small town, it was a relatively wealthy area. The proximity of a horse racecourse and a recently opened casino provided the bank with ample business and meant

214

the bank frequently had large amounts of cash to match the areas demand.

On the day he planned to carry out the raid he once again went over his scheme, first in his head and then he did a dry run using an old van he had at home. He drove to the bank and parked in the street outside and waited for ten minutes. He had no idea how long it was going to take to actually rob the place but he hoped it would not be much longer than that. The he drove off and timed his journey to the next stop on his planned escape. Satisfied that all was in order he returned home to get himself ready.

Stephen was dressed in all black, looking in the bedroom mirror he smiled and then laughed as he reminded himself of the man from the Milk Tray advert that had run on television. Leaving his house he took a thick leather bikers jacket down from a hook by the back door and a pair of motorcycle riding boots from a hall cupboard and went out to his car. He slung them and a large bag into the rear seat before settling himself in the driver's seat. He gave his home one final look, turned to face the long elegantly laid out drive and started the engine.

The trip to the bank was short, a little over two miles from his home. He pulled up in the same spot he had parked in earlier that day and glanced at his watch.

He was terrified when he entered the bank; he did so at precisely 2.30pm, the time chosen to deliberately coincide with the shift change at the small rural police station, itself over 30 minutes away. It was a Friday, the day before one of the race tracks biggest meetings and the day after the weekly market, the banks safes were as full as they could be.

Taking the money had been relatively straight forward, as was his getaway. He had no doubt that he would have been well filmed by the banks CCTV and a lot of people would have seen him leave the bank and probably noted the number plate of his Audi RS4 estate car but it was a quick vehicle and he was an accomplished driver. His high speed exit from the scene and the next hour saw him cover a considerable distance to a remote forest. Before driving into the forest he pulled into the side and waited for a few moments making sure when he drove in he was not observed.

The track he used was only in frequent use at weekends and over the holiday periods with campers and walkers, being so remote and with plenty of choice closer to towns and villages the probability of meeting a dog walker was almost zero. But never the less he had pulled the car into the trees a short way into the woods and gone back to where the track met the road to sweep his tyre marks with a traditional corn broom he retrieved from the car's ~~huge~~ large boot. Satisfied he had disguised the area sufficiently he got back into the car and drove deep into the forest.

The old stone building he arrived at was set at a slight angle to the track so he had been able to park the car behind the building; whilst far from totally secure it did mean the Audi could not be seen directly from the track.

Once in the building he set about counting and sorting the money, placing a mixed variety of notes into a knapsack and stowing the remainder of the money in a metal case. The case had a combination lock of the sort often found in hotel bedrooms, perhaps not the best system in the world but in the unlikely event of it being found the lock would be good enough to deter attempts to unfasten it.

The case, really a trunk, was in what had once been some sort of pantry just off a rudimentary kitchen. He doubted the case would take much finding but he was banking on no one looking in the building in the first place. Even so, when he first brought the thing to the property he had drilled deep into the stone floor and bolted the case to the floor. Taking it away to try to open the lock was also not going to be a simple task.

Happy that everything was as he wanted he left the building on foot. He was now moving slowly as he made his way deeper into the forest. The forest was mostly level but to reach his next destination on the far side of the woods he had to drop into a shallow valley and cross the stream running through the bottom, thereafter he had made his way uphill. Just before the woods met a major road he had left his Yamaha off road bike, complete with panniers. Despite having made the reverse trip only two days earlier he had needed his GPS to be sure he got to the exact spot. As with the building and the Audi the risk that the bike might be discovered was slim but he was mighty relieved to find it where he had left it.

He stowed the money in the bikes panniers along with the knapsack and pulled the bike out of its hiding place. Thereafter Stephen had ridden hard and fast as he headed south. Three hours after the robbery he left his bike in a multi storey car park, changed his clothes and checked in for the evening flight to Perpignan.

His journey had been completed without a hitch which was why several days later he was gazing out across the Mediterranean contemplating the next steps of his plan.

First on his to do list was to deposit the remainder of the cash he held, for this he needed to go to Andorra. Making sure he could deposit the money where he needed was a complicated task. Not made any easier by the fact the original money was in British Pounds; however, his new Andorran Foundation were happy to take payment in Sterling, provided it was in the form of a Bankers Draft, for that he needed to meet with a man in Toulouse on his way. The price of the Bankers Draft was high but in overall context it was good value as far as Harper was concerned.

Before leaving for Toulouse he shaved the now full beard he had grown and washed out the temporary hair colour he had been using.

The trip to Andorra and the transactions involved took the whole of the day and on returning to the rented cottage Stephen was close to exhaustion. His energy levels were falling on an almost daily basis. He planned to have a few quiet days before taking the next steps of his plan. He needed the rest.

He spent a several enjoyable days walking down into Port Vendres, taking a stroll around the walk made famous by Scottish architect and artist Charles Rennie-Mackintosh, stopping to admire copies of his work. He would stop for simple lunches of freshly caught fish and locally grown fresh salad, more than once consuming a sufficient amount of a particularly crisp dry Côtes du Roussillon to require a taxi for the short trip back to his lodgings.

By day six of his interlude Stephen Harper was feeling refreshed. Despite his sense that the medication he was taking was of limited or even no use he diligently stuck to the regime set by his doctor.

The two day old copies of the English papers he managed to come by carried little about the robbery and what there was had now moved deep into the paper. Nothing had appeared in the French papers. He had no access to the internet and Port Vendres did not run to an internet café so he had no chance to look things up online. Fortunately he did have access to a telephone.

The final stages of his plan were very simple. First he needed to complete his letter to the authorities and the newspapers back home and get them in the mail. Then he had a couple of important telephone calls to make. Once both these things had been done he could head to his small flat in Zurich.

As he began to write Stephen Harper was shocked how straight forward, in fact easy, the robbery had been to carry out. So much so he thought his letters should include not only the reasons why he had carried out his crime but an explanation of how that at least might help prevent further robberies. Harper had not carried out his bank robbery because he needed money, he wasn't a career criminal, he was just an ordinary individual with a long memory and a deep desire for some sort of justice and restitution.

To outline his reasons he needed to reflect on the events of the past, for him it was critical to set out what had motivated him to carry out a bank robbery.

Over twenty five years earlier, before he became very successful and substantially wealthy, Harper had been a customer of Central Counties Bank. His fledgling business had begun to generate small profits and allowed him the luxury of savings. On the recommendation of the bank he invested in a scheme that resulted in him losing most of his money. At first he was fairly sanguine and simply put the loss down to a learning experience and got on with his life. It was several months later that he came across a small article in a national newspaper that gave him a shock. Central Counties Bank had access to more information about the investment scheme than they had chosen to disclose to him, in fact the Bank would or should have known full well that the scheme in which he invested was at best unsuitable and at worst downright fraudulent.

Despite complaints to the Bank and the authorities no form of apology or compensation was forthcoming. The cost of legal action was too prohibitive so he was stuck. Among the many victims was a well known local charity that supported under privileged children in the area. Operating on a shoe string the charity had invested a third of their funds in the same scheme, they too were unable to secure recompense. That the charity had survived and still continued to the present day had not left Harper feeling any less angry about the bank and its scheme and he vowed when the time was right to seek justice primarily for the charity and a sense of satisfaction for himself. He had always assumed that would be by legal means.

Things changed substantially for him when less than a year before the robbery he learned that he was terminally ill, he was likely to be able to live quite normally for a number of months but would become increasingly tired as his illness started to take its maximum effect.

He could expect his last few weeks, possibly months, to be extremely difficult and doubtless to require palliative care. His shock and terror at the news left him distraught for a number of days until reflecting on his life Central Counties Bank came to mind. He was amazed as to how upset he became at the thought that he would not now be able to achieve his aim of justice for the wrong the bank had done. That was when the idea to rob the bank came to him. He had nothing to lose, he cared not for his liberty, he had no need for the money, but he did want to bring the whole torrid mess to a satisfactory conclusion. His medical consultant had told him having something to aim for during his last months could help him emotionally and so his plan was hatched. For the first time in a while he had something to live for. A purpose.

The letter explaining his actions and the truth that lay behind them went simultaneously to the bank and a long term friend, a journalist with The Times in London. He had a copy ready to go to the police.

It had been a slow period for news and so receiving his friend's correspondence was a welcome interruption. However the contents had not only startled Simon Arbuthnot but created extreme excitement and utter disbelief in equal measure. When the mail arrived Arbuthnot had been seated in his small study at the rear of his home overlooking his well tended narrow garden that ran down to a canal tow path. He had been day dreaming staring into the middle distance, lost in another world. What he should have been doing was finishing a short piece for a monthly magazine about a protest group created to stop the spread of fracking for shale gas in southern England. Freya, his pet spaniel, brought him to his senses as the post hit the front door mat; neither had heard the approaching postman.

Like most folk Arbuthnot's mail was largely junk consisting of double glazing sales material, charity requests and offers from solar panel fitting companies. He quickly tossed them all to one side and stopped when he saw the handwritten envelope with a French postage stamp. He picked the letter up and was immediately curious about the French postage and of course a handwritten envelope, hardly anyone sent a letter at all these days let alone handwritten. He quickly opened it to discover the letter inside was typed, only the address on the envelope being written, before reading it he turned to the last page of the letter to see it had been sent by Stephen Harper. They had not been in contact for a couple of years and Stephen Harper was not a man taken to writing previously and now he had sent a letter several pages long. Intrigued, Arbuthnot left the rest of his mail and walked back to his study to read it.

The very same day Simon Arbuthnot received Harpers letter he began trying to contact his old friend, calling different land line and mobile phone numbers, leaving messages all to no avail. He was becoming quite agitated, for he knew if the story in Harpers letter was true then he had the story of the year, perhaps of his career.

Sitting at his desk Arbuthnot went again through every number and possible contact that could help him reach Harper. He had twice hit his desk in frustration, he knew fine well that someone who had robbed a bank was unlikely to be handy to reach but he was desperate to write his story. When his own mobile phone rang he was so startled he let it ring several times before he could answer, when he did the shock was even greater.

"Simon?" the voice at the other end asked.

"Yes."

"Simon, it's Stephen Harper," came the reply, the silence was as loud as any exclamation could be, Harper heard his old friends breathing, it was rushed almost ragged.

"Is that you Stephen?" a brief pause before he added, "is... it... Where are you?"

"It's me and I'm sorry but I can't tell you where I am. Did you get my letter?" Arbuthnot's reply was almost chocked, "Yes"

"Good, I was worried it might not reach you," said Harper

"Bloody hell Stephen, I can hardly believe it's you," he paused for a moment, "your letter, is it true?" he asked.

"Yes, Simon every last word."

"Wow, it's... Well, surreal. I'm not sure my editor will entirely believe it."

"Simon, I do need to ask you one favour though, please do not publish this for three days."

"You can't give me a story like this and ask me not to run it Stephen, what if someone else gets it? The bloody police are bound to publish it..." Arbuthnot sounded exasperated.

"Don't worry, their copy hasn't been sent yet, I have a couple of things to do first."

"So what is your plan?"

~~So~~ Harper told him.

Harper was oddly nervous about the next step in his plan; why, he didn't know, but his stomach was churning, he felt quite sick. His call to the head office of Central Counties bank was instantly put through to the Chief Executive's secretary, it was clear she did not fully believe the purpose of the call assuming Harper to be a crank, however his calm persuasiveness was sufficient for her to put him on hold. He was left waiting a while presumably as she spoke to her boss and they debated the merits of the call.

A full five minutes later she came back on the line. "Mr Blackstock will speak to you now," she said. Harper detected a faint digital buzz as his call was transferred.

"Mr Harper?" said the voice on the other end of the line. "This is David Blackstock, how can I help you?"

"Well Mr Blackstock, as I am sure your secretary has told you, I am the man who robbed your bank."

"So you say Mr Harper, but you don't really expect me to believe that do you?"

"I can understand why you might be sceptical Mr Blackstock, after all not many people who rob a bank would want to call the bank in question and confess," Harper replied. "But ask yourself this, if I am not the person who robbed your bank what possible reason could I have for calling?"

"As I say Mr Harper, a crank."

"Really?" said Harper, the question in his tone rising like the singing voice of a 1950's crooner. "Do I sound cranky to you, slightly unhinged perhaps or irrational?"

"Oddly you do not, in fact your voice sounds quite…" He hesitated, searching for the most appropriate word, "Quite rational actually, but that still does not convince me."

There was a few moments silence as Harper allowed the banker to think.

"Ok Mr Blackstock, can I ask you a question?" Again he paused. "Did you receive a letter with a French postmark? If you did then you must know I must be the person who sent it."

"Frankly Harper, I think it is time to terminate this call," Blackstock replied, his irritation becoming clear. "I have indulged you long enough, I have a business to run and need to get on."

Harper could hear Blackstock moving in his chair presumably in the throes of hanging up the call. Quickly he asked, "What if I said "Guaranteed Deposit Equity Bond?"

Blackstock hesitated, there was an audible intake of breath, it could have been Blackstock losing further patience with his caller or as Harper suspected an intake of breath caused by surprise.

"Should that mean something to me?" Blackstock asked.

"I am sure it does Mr Blackstock, surely you must remember the product that guaranteed your elevation to a senior post in the bank and ultimately to Central Counties board?" He paused briefly. "The product that in 1985 produced the bulk of the bank's profits, a product that had begun well for both the bank and its customers but sadly a product that in the end the bank began to rely on to produce profit." Again he paused briefly. "Surely you must remember that, after all you have been with the bank for 35 years I think, is that not true?"

"Yes of course I have been here a long time but you can't expect me to remember every last detail of every product we have provided our customers in that time," Blackstock responded.

"Actually Mr Blackstock I do not expect you to remember every product but this one I am sure you must remember." Again he paused. "I don't think you are being entirely straight with me Mr Blackstock, something you have been quite adept at over the years. You were in charge of selling investments and insurance at the bank in the late 1980's weren't you Mr Blackstock?"

"I was that's true," replied Blackstock, a note of caution creeping into his previously steady voice. "But so what if I was?"

"It's simple really, you see your bank sold me and others an investment scheme that you claimed provided a guaranteed return and yet it only resulted in me losing my money, when I complained you miraculously produced a letter supposedly given to me explaining that the investment was not guaranteed. A letter I never received."

"Mr Harper I really cannot see there is any point continuing this conversation, you have confessed to stealing a great deal of money from this bank and I as its head I must do all I can to both secure the return of the money and of course see to it that you are brought before the Courts. Given that I have a letter not only telling me you committed the crime but also how you did it I can only assume you are in fact happy to be caught, so why not make this a lot easier and tell me where you are and where the money is?" As his confidence grew Blackstock began to sound increasingly pompous.

Stephen drew in a long breath and held it for a few moments as he considered his response.

"Well?" interrupted Blackstock.

"I really don't think you are in a position to make demands Mr Blackstock," Stephen replied. "In fact only I can do that as it is me that has the money" Harper paused again allowing several moments of silence to build. "I have a deal to offer you Mr Blackstock... You see we both know you acted badly at the time the bank sold the Guaranteed Deposit Equity Bond, don't we? What's more your actions in covering your tracks at the bank might well be considered fraudulent. We also know that if you did something similar today the regulators would see to it that compensation be paid to investors and that you would be prevented from working in financial services again."

It was Blackstock's turn to remain silent.

"So here is the deal Mr Blackstock, you are to make a donation as compensation to the children's charity you swindled. I suggest an amount that would cover the lost investment plus interest with a little uplift for good measure. As soon as you have arranged the gift you will tender your resignation. In return I will not tell the newspapers about your part in covering up the ~~misspelling~~ misselling of the Bonds and I will tell the Police where the money is. If you do not, you will be embroiled in scandal."

"You cannot prove anything against me," countered Blackstock.

"No I can't, you are quite right, but for the newspapers to cause you serious trouble I don't need to be able to prove a thing. Do you really want the pressure the papers could bring? Imagine if you cracked under the pressure and the truth came out?" Harper paused to let his questions sink in.

"I think we both know Mr Blackstock that a quiet exit stage left would be very much in your best interests, don't we?"

After his call to Blackstock Simon Harper prepared for the next stage of his plan by making his second appointment with a clinic in Zurich which specialises in helping the terminally ill take their own lives. He arranged an appointment two days hence with their doctors. He had first met them the week before he carried out the robbery at Central Counties Bank so they could assess both his physical and mental health, the latter being crucial to ensure he had full capacity to make the momentous step of ending his own life. On that occasion he had left a full copy of his medical notes with the doctors for them to consider.

His next action was to arrange travel to Zurich, given his wealth and the lack of time he had left with which to use it he arranged for a private jet to collect him from Perpignan airport for the trip to Zurich.

Once his reservation was complete he contacted his lawyer and explained what he needed before heading out for the walk down to Port Vendres. He was both delighted with the superb views and distraught that he would not see them again. He fully intended to enjoy his stay.

Finding his way through the busy throng around the harbour and marina Harper took his pre reserved seat at the town's most celebrated fish restaurant. Although he read the menu he had pretty much decided what he would choose. To begin he ordered a dozen of the finest oysters and for his main course a fresh lobster. To complement his meal he had previously requested a fine wine that was not on the restaurants normal list. The wine he knew cost the equivalent of a transatlantic airfare, but for Harper the price was an irrelevance, he was only interested in its wonderful taste and qualities. The wine he had chosen was a 2005 Pouilly-Fume Silex by Didier Dagueneau. It's rarity such that it had taken the restaurant several weeks to source a bottle.

Harper's meal was simply delicious; the salty taste of the sea from his oyster's bringing back memories of many happy days of family holidays when he was first introduced to the delicacies of shell fish. The lobster was excellent also, he could not decide whether it was the best he had ever eaten or if merely the setting and excellent wine came together to cause the ultimate in gastronomic sensation. Either way he was for the moment at least a truly happy and satisfied man.

He left not only a generous tip but a third of the bottle of wine giving the patron clear instruction that all his staff should have the chance to try a wine that they could never hope to afford for themselves.

The remaining forty-eight hours in Port Vendres passed both without incident and blissfully quiet. His plans were not ruined by a knock on the door by the

233

local Police and he was soon packing his few belongings and heading by taxi to Perpignan airport. The flight to Zurich was relatively short and less than two hours after boarding his private charter Stephen Harper was walking through the VIP customs hall at Zurich airport, from there he was taken to his lakeside apartment ahead of his appointment at the clinic.

His next appointment was crucial, this was the stage where he would learn whether or not the clinic had decided to accept him and assuming they had a time at which he would be expected to complete a great deal of legal paperwork. Given the pleasantness of the weather Harper chose to walk to the clinic, one last chance to enjoy the waterside of the Zurichsee.

From Harper's view point his appointment went extremely well and although somewhat lengthy he left in the knowledge that his next trip would be his last.

The day after his appointment with the clinic Harper set about the final preparations of his plan to gain justice for the charity. As he had promised in a recent call to his lawyer he sent by courier two separate packages, neither was to be opened until the day after his death and then only one of them was to be opened. The package to be opened would be determined by the news or otherwise of David Blackstock's resignation and that the children's charity had received a most unexpected donation from Central Counties bank.

If the conditions set by Harper were met, then an envelope containing a full confession by Harper of his crime and a map detailing the whereabouts of the money was to be opened and the relevant information passed to the police. If they were not met, then the second package should be opened. This also contained the same information as the first, with the addition of an explanation of why he had carried out his crime and an instruction that Simon Arbuthnot should receive this for him to release his story.

Satisfied that he was now fully prepared Harper once again called Central Counties bank, his call was passed to David Blackstock without hesitation on this occasion and the news that greeted Harper was to him at least very satisfying as Blackstock had agreed to the demands.

Although satisfied Stephen still did not trust Blackstock so to make sure his demands were met he had arranged for the bank to issue the notice of Blackstock's resignation to all news channels and online media simultaneously and he told Blackstock only when that was done would he release the details of where he had hidden the money and the combination to unlock the metal case. He was expecting the call from his lawyer that afternoon.

When it came the call startled Stephen, he had been sleeping, the steady onset of the tiredness kept taking him by surprise. He had been reading, or rather re reading an old favourite book of spying intrigue by John Le Carre when he had dozed off. He had been falling asleep most afternoons for the last week or so but each day the tiredness came quicker. He was increasingly terrified by the pace of its onset. Gathering himself he stood and picked up his mobile phone.

"Stephen Harper," he announced, his old telephone answering habits from years of work firmly ingrained.

"Hello Stephen, it's Godfrey Bainbridge," the voice at the other end announced. Godfrey had been Harpers corporate lawyer for many years. As his business success had out grown the capability of the traditional small firm he used when he started his career he had been recommended to Godfrey, who at the time was a newly created partner in a substantial London based firm. Now in his late sixties and still hard at it Godfrey Bainbridge was the senior partner. They had become firm friends and the call that Bainbridge was now making was the most difficult call he had ever made.

"Hello Godfrey, how are you?" asked Stephen.

Bainbridge was almost totally lost for words and struggled to respond. "Stephen I am fine, it just... Well I have no idea what to say."

"That's alright Godfrey, please don't worry, there is nothing anyone can do and it does come to us all in the end you know. Now before we start getting too emotional, what news?"

"Well, good news I guess. I have just had notice of Blackstock's resignation and I have checked it with the BBC business news and also it has been announced to the financial regulators."

"Excellent Godfrey, excellent."

"There is more though Stephen, running along announcement was a small piece concerning a large donation made to a children's charity."

With this last bit of news ringing in his ears, Stephen Harper felt a tiny amount of moisture in his eyes. He sniffed quickly to prevent the onset of tears and more emotion than he felt fair to impose on his friend.

"Godfrey, thank you. That is the best news I have had in a very long time."

"Stephen it's ok, I just wish the circumstances were otherwise."

"I know old friend I know. You are already to release the papers from my first package I hope."

"Yes I am, although it troubles me a great deal."

"Godfrey, I don't want to be rude, but before emotions get the better of me, I just want to say thank you and good bye old friend."

"Good bye Stephen."

Harper did not wait or say anything further, he hung up the phone and turned back to the window of his apartment. He stared at the distant mountain tops and began to cry like he had never cried before. As the emotion threatened to overwhelm him he sat down and put his head in his hands.

It was some while before he recovered himself and as he did a broad smile broke across his face. Stephen was not upset at nearing the end, he was more happy with the outcome for the charity than he had been for anything else in his life.